I saw the silhouette of a man off to my left.

"What is it Charlie?" I asked, turning to look over my shoulder.

There was no one there.

Great. Now I was imagining things.

And I was missing the shades of sunlight on the water.

Feeling cross, I dipped my brush into a darker blue and blended it onto the paint already on my canvas.

Deciding that the shade I had just created worked better for the sky, I moved my attention there. The morning sunlight on the misty clouds were pretty, but I quickly did what I did. I changed up what I saw to make it look better on the canvas. Put my own spin on what I was seeing.

And pretty soon I was mixing all sorts of blues together.

I decided I would call this one Lavender Blue.

I saw the man out of the corner of my eyes again. I sat very still. He was a tall, lean man. Wearing some sort of uniform with an odd round hat. His hair was short and he was clean-shaven.

He wasn't Charlie or Drake or Thomas. He wasn't my brother either.

I set my paint brush down very slowly and turned quickly.

But the second I turned, the man vanished.

What the—?

Deciding I had done enough painting for one day—perhaps too many paint fumes—I gathered everything up. Packed in my shoulder bag. I didn't like it that my hands were trembling.

LAVENDER BLUE

Falling Through to Forever

LAVENDER BLUE

THE BECQUERELS

KATHRYN KALEIGH

LAVENDER BLUE

CHAMPAGNE SILVER PREVIEW

To learn more about Kathryn Kaleigh, visit

www.kathrynkaleigh.com

Kathryn Kaleigh

PROLOGUE

"Graham Daniels."

Graham adjusted his mortarboard, sweeping the tassel off his cheek, and took his turn to walk across the formal stage. His professors and classmates were all here along with several hundred strangers.

The graduation ceremony was a rite of passage for most.

For Graham, it was something more.

"Let's step up here for a moment, Graham," Dr. Quinn, the president of the little Pittsburg college instructed.

A bit baffled, he followed Dr. Quinn to the podium. "I just wanted to let everyone know that Graham was voted by his classmates… and professors, too, I might add, as the one most likely to succeed."

Graham flinched. This wasn't something he wanted. He wanted to just blend in with everyone else. If he'd known this was going to happen, he would have skipped graduation and went straight to his new job. Could have had his diploma mailed.

But, of course, he smiled, shook Dr. Quinn's hand, and took his diploma.

He did not need the extra attention drawn to himself.

Everyone already knew that by all rights, he wasn't supposed to be here.

CHAPTER 1
GRAHAM DANIELS

I stepped outside onto the front porch of my little log cabin and surveyed my land.

Today was a beautiful springtime day. Nice and cool this morning with a promise of showers in the afternoon, like every afternoon. A warm afternoon followed by a chilly night.

A burbling river ran behind the cabin, making its way over huge boulders creating a rush of water that lulled me to sleep at night. Fragrant spruce and fir trees scattered around the house was home to chipmunks and birds.

I lived side by side in perfect harmony with all animals. Elk. Bears. Big horn sheep.

A two-lane blacktop road ran about twenty yards from my front porch. From about seven o'clock in the morning to about eight o'clock at night, it was alive with cars and buses carrying hikers and tourists and photographers out to get an up close look at the splendor of the Rocky Mountain National Park.

Across the road, across the meadow, stood the mountains. From here I could see Long's Peak. Always identifiable by the way the rocks resembled a giant beaver climbing up the side of the peak.

Okay. Not technically my land, but it was my job to oversee it.

One of five other full-time National Park rangers, I was the only one who wanted to actually live inside the park. Besides, Maggie, but she didn't count. She'd been here forever. When my predecessor retired, this cabin came up for grabs.

I considered myself most fortunate that no one higher in seniority than me wanted it.

It was perfect. I could live without nosy neighbors. No television. No cell phone service. Just me and nature.

Of course, I had work. That meant I had to routinely lead nature walks. Hikes. Campfire programs. Those didn't bother me. I didn't mind getting out and doing things. I wasn't a recluse. I just preferred to spend my time off alone.

But today was going to be an easy day. Today I had no assignments. On days like this I was allowed to just walk whatever trail I wanted to walk. Explore. Make sure there were no problems. Wear my uniform and answer questions.

Since it was only my third day on the job, I decided I would hike up to Bierstadt Lake. Check out the trail. See if any maintenance was needed. Since it was one of the trails assigned to me, it seemed like a good one to start off with. Well-traveled. Well loved. An easy hike.

I made myself a latte. A graduation present from myself to myself. It would take a while to get the city out of me. In the meantime, I gave myself a few small pleasures and lattes happened to be one of them.

Took my latte out on the back porch and sat on the one big wooden chair that had come with the place.

I watched the river racing over the rocks. It didn't know it was racing ahead to a waterfall about a mile from here.

Sort of like life, I mused. We raced headlong forward, not having a clue what we were racing toward. *Can't wait for the weekend to get here. Be so glad when this semester is over.* So many people never even lived to see that weekend or the end of that semester. If they knew, perhaps they would slow down, enjoy the day they were in. But instead, we all just raced blindly along toward our waterfalls.

I filled my backpack with bottles of water, granola bars, my park issued satellite phone.

I packed three extra small bottles of water in case I happened across a dehydrated tourist or two.

Added in a notepad and a camera. This was work and I took it seriously.

Just because I happened to love what I did, didn't make me any less responsible. On the contrary.

I took my park ranger truck to the Bear Lake trailhead and parked at the far end of the parking lot. Didn't want to take up a spot someone else might need. If it hadn't been so far from my cabin, I would have just walked.

I took the trail around Bear Lake first. The most popular hike in the park, it was well maintained with little wooden bridges that made perfect photo backgrounds. Everything seemed to be in order. It was early yet, so not too many tourists. The ranger manning the information booth wasn't even here yet.

After the quick hike around Bear Lake, I veered off onto the Bierstadt Lake trail. The first part of the trail was straight up. I was in good shape, but my breath coming in a bit labored reminded me to take it easy since I hadn't had time to adapt to the elevation yet.

I kept my jacket zipped as I headed up the trail. Even with the change in elevation, it was cooler the higher I went.

I moved quickly over the rocky trail, enjoying the aloneness.

I was in a unique position that I tried not to think about.

It was coming up on the one-year anniversary.

Reaching an area where the park engineers had put bridges

on the trail for people to walk on, it looked like I was walking over mist.

I stopped. Grabbed my camera out of the side pocket of my backpack and took a couple of photos. It was beautiful here. There was always a new way to see things and the weather had so much to do with those changes.

The trail leveled off as I neared the lake. I took a couple of notes. Things that could be better. A loose handrail on one of the bridges. A broken step.

When I reached the banks of the lake, I sat on a boulder at the edge of the water and ate a granola bar.

I was the only person here, but I was certain that would change before long.

Mist hovered over the lake, giving it a magical look.

I remembered this lake from when I was a teen. This was one of the good memories. It was odd how the bad memories made the good memories sad. It was like a misery loves company thing.

But I fought it. I fought against those bad memories, doing my best to keep the bad from tainting the good.

It was hard. I readily admitted that to myself.

The light shifted and the mist vanished from the lake.

Sunlight glinted off the water, blinding me for a second.

Deciding to take a walk around the lake, I stashed my water bottle and wrapper in my backpack and left my boulder. But I decided to take a photo first. As a park ranger, I never knew when I might need pictures. My favorite professor had been old-school. He had taught me that.

I hiked toward the right, quickly reaching an open area on the west side of the lake.

My feet froze to the ground.

I saw a beautiful young lady with long brunette hair falling loosely around her shoulders, barely held back by a loosely tied bow.

She wore a long light blue dress with long sleeves and a high neck. A long dress. As in it billowed out around her where she sat on the ground.

She didn't see me. Her focus was intent on the canvas in front of her. The paint canvas was propped on a little stand and she held a palette of colors in her right hand while she splashed paint onto the canvas with her left.

I looked away. Across the lake. Squeezed my eyes tightly closed.

This was... unexpected. I thought the visions had stopped. It had been a long time since it had happened. And not like this.

I looked back. The girl was still there. I could see her profile now. She was quite lovely. Beautiful actually.

I stared at her longer than I should have. Longer than would have been polite if she was a real person. Longer than I should entertain a vision.

My therapist had taught me better.

Not wanting to look away, but dutifully doing it anyway, I turned around this time. Counted to ten. Then counted to ten again.

The girl should be gone now.

I turned back. Looked in the direction where the girl had been.

Had been.

She was gone now.

But I did not want her to be gone.

I did not want her to be one of my visions.

CHAPTER 2
BAILEY AUCLAIR

1867

I'd had to slip off in the early morning to get some time alone.

Not that I particularly wanted to be alone. I just needed alone time to get any painting done.

It made me a bit cross to have to literally get up with the chickens in order to get that alone time.

But Charlie Jackson followed me around like a puppy. Then there was Drake Lafleur. Drake was a bit older and didn't like me going off without a chaperone. Somehow he seemed to think he was exempt and it was okay for me to go off with him. Like he was my chaperone.

And there was Thomas Beaumont.

I put all three of them out of my mind and focused on getting the hues of the water just right. The reflection of the sun was magical right now. But in just a few minutes, the angle of the sun would change and the hues would be completely different.

Something behind me caught my attention.

I hadn't told anyone I was coming up here, but everyone knew it was my favorite place to come and paint when the weather was right.

It was only a fifteen-minute walk from my back door, so it wasn't far. I didn't see any danger in it. Besides, I knew how to protect myself.

I saw the silhouette of a man off to my left.

"What is it Charlie?" I asked, turning to look over my shoulder.

There was no one there.

Great. Now I was imagining things.

And I was missing the shades of sunlight on the water.

Feeling cross, I dipped my brush into a darker blue and blended it onto the paint already on my canvas.

Deciding that the shade I had just created worked better for the sky, I moved my attention there. The morning sunlight on the misty clouds were pretty, but I quickly did what I did. I changed up what I saw to make it look better on the canvas. Put my own spin on what I was seeing.

And pretty soon I was mixing all sorts of blues together.

I decided I would call this one Lavender Blue.

I saw the man out of the corner of my eyes again. I sat very still. He was a tall, lean man. Wearing some sort of uniform with an odd round hat. His hair was short and he was clean-shaven.

He wasn't Charlie or Drake or Thomas. He wasn't my brother either.

I set my paint brush down very slowly and turned quickly.

But the second I turned, the man vanished.

What the—?

Deciding I had done enough painting for one day—perhaps too many paint fumes—I gathered everything up. Packed in my shoulder bag. I didn't like it that my hands were trembling.

My sister, Andrea, was married to a man who had appeared

out of nowhere, then vanished before coming back to stay. She never talked about it, but she didn't have to. I knew.

I knew more than people gave me credit for. I'd learned a long time ago that a smile and a carefully timed blink of the eyes could get me pretty much anything I wanted.

For example, Thomas had agreed to ride into Boulder City to pick up a bolt of material I had ordered for a new dress. I could have it sent here, but that would add on an additional week and I wanted to get it to the seamstress so she could have it ready before the dance next weekend.

There were definitely perks to knowing how to use a smile and a gaze. It wasn't my fault that all girls didn't know how to do that.

I was trying to teach my little sister, Elise, but she was kind of goofy and just ended up giggling. She didn't care about boys. At least not yet. She was still young.

I walked quickly as I followed the little dirt trail home.

I felt unsettled. I'd felt like I was being watched which in itself didn't bother me so much, but having that feeling when there was no one there was the definition of insanity.

I might be a free-spirited artist and all that, but I did not consider myself to be insane.

"What's wrong with you?" Dakota asked when I came in through the back door and went into the parlor.

"Nothing," I said.

Dakota narrowed her eyes at me. "Doesn't look like nothing," she said.

Dakota was the complete opposite of my younger sister Elise. Dakota was suspicious of everyone and nothing got past her.

If something was going on, Dakota would know it.

"The sunlight was wrong," I lied. It had actually been a beautiful morning.

Dakota glanced out the window. "Looks like a perfect day for painting."

I huffed out a breath.

"I got spooked. Okay?"

"Animal?"

"I don't know." I dropped onto the sofa, setting my bag down at my feet and propping my still slightly wet painting next to it. "Where's everybody?" I asked, decided that distraction was my best defense.

"Elise is upstairs napping and Colton is out doing whatever Colton does."

"Right. Any letters?"

She knew I was asking if we had gotten a letter from our oldest sister Andrea who lived in Denver.

"No letters," she said. "Maybe you'll tell me later what happened out there." She picked up her book and opened it.

"Good." I crossed my arms and sat back.

Hector, our small, older Chinese butler brought me tray with a pitcher of water and some little cubes of fresh cheese.

I thanked him and filled a glass with water. Glanced over at Dakota.

I hadn't wanted to talk about what I had seen out there, but now that I was home and settled, I kind of did. I'd never been one to keep things to myself for very long.

Dakota caught me staring at her and set her book aside. "I thought Thomas was going with you," she said.

"I told him I changed my mind about going. I wanted some alone time to actually paint." Besides, Thomas was handsy. I had no trouble deflecting him. But it took all my attention, making painting next to impossible.

"Can I see it?" she asked.

Dakota and I had never been particularly close. Dakota and Andrea had always been the close ones, but now that Andrea lived in Denver, Dakota was more affable toward her other siblings.

"Of course." I lifted the painting and held it up by the edges. "I'm calling it Lavender Blue," I said.

"When did you start naming your paintings?" she asked.

"All the great artists name their paintings. It's a thing."

"I've never heard of a great artist who paints a new one every day."

"Well. Now you have," I said, feigning offense. Actually, I was pleased that she noticed I finished a painting at least every other day. "I can't help it if I'm prolific."

"I think they're great because they aren't prolific. If everyone had an original, how could they be valuable?"

I just stared at Dakota. She had surely lost her mind. Maybe she just didn't understand.

"Besides, won't you run out of names?" she asked.

"That's silly. I'll never run out of names." I popped a cube of cheese into my mouth. But now she had me thinking. What if I was painting too much? Maybe I'd switch to charcoals for awhile.

"I don't see anything that looks spooky about your painting," she said, circling back around to why I had looked startled when I got home.

"It's nothing you can see, Silly," I said.

Maybe I wouldn't talk about it after all.

CHAPTER 3
GRAHAM

I tossed a frozen pizza into the oven, then sat down at my computer and transferred the photos I had taken from my camera onto the bigger computer screen.

After scrolling impatiently through the first pictures I had taken, I slowed down when I got to the ones of the lake itself.

I tried zooming in, but the angle was wrong. I couldn't see the clearing where I had seen the girl.

I zoomed in anyway. There. I could just see a shadow.

The timer dinged for my pizza so I pushed back in my chair and stood up.

A few minutes later, I brought the plate with pizza back to my desk and studied the photo.

The shadow could be anything.

It *could* belong to the girl. I refused to own the vision.

My therapist had called the visions daymares.

And the daymares were unpleasant to say the least. The girl I had seen was beautiful. Good. Positive.

Sitting back, absently eating my cheese pizza, I considered calling my therapist. I could call him anytime. He would know —might know—how to explain what I had seen.

He'd probably say something like *you're feeling more like yourself. Seeing a positive future. This is a good thing.*

I didn't want to hear that. I didn't want her to be a sign that I was moving forward. I mean, I wanted to move forward, I just didn't her to be a sign of it.

I wanted her to be a real person.

I had not dated anyone since… almost a year ago.

Hadn't even wanted to so much as look at a woman.

I flipped through the other pictures I had taken of the lake. Somehow I had managed to skip the angle that would have been required to see where she had been sitting.

I would go back up there. That was it. I simply had to go back.

This wasn't the kind of thing that a man could just brush off. Especially not a man with my history.

My landline rang.

A few minutes later, I hung up the phone.

I wouldn't be going back up there today. Today I had to fill in for one of the other rangers. His wife was having a baby and the baby was coming today.

Unfortunately that particular ranger had a busy calendar. Since I was the new guy, they hadn't wanted to overwhelm me.

But that had just changed.

Circumstances dictated that I be overwhelmed.

If I hadn't wanted to go back to the lake to look for the girl so much, I wouldn't have minded. At least maybe being busy would help keep my mind off the possibility that I had had a setback.

It was not, however, keeping my mind off the girl. Figment of my imagination or not, I couldn't stop thinking about her.

There was no way in hell I was telling my therapist that.

It wouldn't be long though before I headed back up there.

I wanted to face this one head on.

CHAPTER 4
BAILEY

I sat on a boulder next to the roaring mountain river, my sketchpad in my lap, deftly wielding a piece of charcoal in my left hand.

It was one of those lazy Sunday afternoons with perfect weather. Warm sun and cool breeze.

The light breeze tousled the hair I had tied back loosely to keep it from flying everywhere.

Charlie, the youngest of my beaus, sat a few feet away, leaning back on his elbows, his face turned up to the sun. I think he might be nearly asleep.

Thomas, standing several yards away at the edge of the river bank, cast a fishing line into the water. It seemed rather ridiculous to think that he would catch something in such cold, rushing water.

Drake sat a few feet away on my other side, his attention on the open pages of a book.

Sitting by the river had been one of my inspirational ideas. The river was too loud for more than limited conversation.

So I was able to sketch in peace.

The three men typically called on me separately, but this

was the third Sunday they had all shown up on the same afternoon.

It was baffling to me that they didn't seem to mind. They, in fact, seemed to get along with each other quite well.

I did not have an exclusive relationship with any of them, leaving them all three to call on me at their whim.

I was quite good at deflecting them away from any seriousness because, quite frankly, I did not care to marry any of them. At some point, I might choose one of them or I might not. Since I did not need to marry for money, I felt no pressure to look for a husband.

I lived with two of my sisters and my brother. We owned our home outright and each of us had enough money to last us most of our lifetimes if we were frugal.

Frugality could well be my downfall. I spent a lot of money on canvas and painting supplies. I also liked fashion.

It pained me that my copies of Godey's Ladies Book were already out of style by the time they reached me out here on the frontier.

So my fashion was about one step behind the rest of the world.

I liked it here in Whiskey Springs, Colorado in spite of that.

The war had broken out just as I was coming of age, sending the majority of eligible bachelors to the battle lines and too many of them had not come back.

One of those who had not come back was our father. It was by chance we learned that he had purchased a home in Whiskey Springs with the plan of moving his wife and five children away from the battle scarred south once the war was over.

Unfortunately, our mother had not lived long after Father had been killed.

I added a few strokes to the mountain top I was working on. Stopped and looked over at Charlie.

"Have you ever noticed that it looks like a giant beaver climbing up the side of the peak?"

Charlie opened his eyes. Looked toward Longs Peak, considering. Then he laughed. "It does, doesn't it? Only an artist's eye could see that." He looked over at me with admiration.

I smiled back at him, then went back to my sketching.

"I'm going to climb that mountain one day," Thomas said over his shoulder.

"You are not," I said, laughing.

"I am," he said. "There's a group of people in Boulder City who meet once a month to prepare."

"Prepare how?" Drake asked, setting his book aside.

"Learning how to tie knots and how to climb. Technical stuff. I'm going to start going," Thomas said.

I wiped my fingers on my apron and focused on Thomas for a minute. I'd always seen Thomas as the wildest one of my beaus. The most foolhardy.

Him talking about climbing up to the top of a rugged mountaintop set off alarm bells for me. Not that I was ready to get married. But if I did decide to marry, I would want a steady, reliable man who would be there for me.

A foolhardy man who needed to run off and make dangerous climbs up mountains would not make a good husband.

I filed that piece of information away in the back of my mind and picked up my piece of charcoal again.

I wanted to finish this sketch today. It didn't matter that Dakota thought I was doing too many paintings and sketches. Surely there could never be too many. Besides, I didn't care. I liked doing it.

As I sketched in a scattering of fluffy clouds behind the mountain peaks, my thoughts strayed back to my experience at Bierstadt Lake.

I know I had seen a man standing there watching me. I had seen him just as clear as I saw Charlie on my left and Drake on my right.

But when I turned to look directly at them, they did not vanish.

I was going to go back up there.

I thought about taking one of the guys with me, but I quickly discarded that thought. If I said the word, all three of them would go with me right now.

But it would not do to take one man with me when I was going looking for another.

No. That would not do at all.

CHAPTER 5
GRAHAM

*I*t was Saturday before I could get back to Bierstadt Lake. And as luck would have it, it was not only my day off, it was the anniversary.

A good day to take a hike. Better than staying home alone. Spending my time trying to distract myself.

I decided not to wear my ranger uniform. Instead I put on a pair of comfortable jeans and t-shirt, layering a sweatshirt over it. Since my park issued boots were best for hiking, I wore them.

I grabbed a Yankee's ball cap and my backpack, then headed out the door.

Another beautiful day in the Rockies.

Nothing at all like that rainy night one year ago today in Pittsburgh.

The Bear Lake parking lot was packed by the time I got there. I circled around and snagged a parking place by Chasm Falls. I preferred to use the trailhead at Bear Lake, but this would have to do. It was something of a walk down to this other Bierstadt Lake trailhead, but I wasn't the only one doing it today.

Then it hit me. This was Memorial Day weekend. I had been so focused on not dwelling on the calendar, trying not to think about what happened a year ago, that it had completely slipped my mind that it was the kickoff weekend to summer.

Damn. They had even talked about that in the last park ranger's meeting.

Somehow I had just blocked it out.

Just went to show how hard I was working on not paying attention to the calendar.

Yet there it was. Despite all my efforts to not know what today was. Burned into my brain. The one year anniversary that changed my life.

An elk looked up as I passed. Twitched his ears, then went back to eating. Apparently he saw me as no threat to him.

I worried that the wild animals were so trusting. Not toward me. But some of the tourists tended to get too close. Closer than was safe.

Just last week a tourist had been gored by a buffalo. Got too close trying to take a selfie. It was so hard not to blame the tourists. But, of course, they were city people. They did not understand just how untamed the animals out here were.

The sun was hot on my back, burning through my t-shirt as I followed the switchbacks up to the top. Around and around. Almost made me dizzy.

I decided I would come back by Bear Lake and walk the road to my truck. Wouldn't be bad. It was all downhill.

Finally, reaching the plateau, I stopped and sat on a fallen log for a rest. I would adjust to the elevation, but it took some time.

After my water and granola bar break, I walked through the trees, making the last leg to Bierstadt Lake.

Clouds were gathering for the typical afternoon shower, casting shadows on everything.

There had been a lot of people on the trail with me, but they had dispersed somewhere and I no longer saw them.

They had gotten ahead of me when I stopped to break.

When I saw the lake peeking through the trees up ahead, I caught my breath. It always amazed me at just how magical it looked.

It was beautiful as always, nestled in a little flat meadow high in the mountains.

Coming in from the opposite direction, I remembered that there was a ghost town not far from here. I couldn't remember the name of it right off hand.

But it had been here, just vanishing, leaving no trace other than the remnants of a couple of cabins.

It was hard to imagine that before this was a national park, there was a full-fledged town here with saloons and a blacksmith and homes.

People had actually lived here in what I suppose had been an older version of what would now be a suburb of Whiskey Springs.

What I wouldn't give to see the town back then. A settlement on this lake. And to have lived here… what a treat it must have been.

As I approached the open area where I had seen the girl in the long dress, my heartrate tripped into high speed.

I was actually nervous. Nervous about seeing what had to be a mythological girl.

It hadn't occurred to me until now, but perhaps I had seen a ghost from the ghost town. That made more sense than me seeing a girl in a daymare. Daymares that I didn't have anymore.

I had put the daymares behind me and I rarely had the nightmares anymore. Bad dreams, on some occasions, yes, but the nightmares were few and far between. The fresh mountain air helped, too.

I stood in the meadow where the girl had been and slowly turned around.

The clouds opened up and a light rain began falling.

So there was rain.

But no girl.

No girl wearing a long dress, putting paint on a canvas.

The disappointment settled over me like a heavy fog.

It was only a light afternoon shower, so I went over and stood beneath a fir tree. Closed my eyes and took deep breaths, let them out slowly.

It was just a bad day for me. That was all.

There was no getting around that.

All in all, I thought I was getting through it rather well.

If nothing else, I was holding my own.

I was here. I was working. I was holding.

I couldn't ask for more from myself. Not now. Maybe not ever.

For a man who wasn't supposed to be here, I thought I was doing about as well as anyone could ask for.

CHAPTER 6
BAILEY

The next morning, I got up, put on my new forest green riding habit and my lace up boots. I wasn't going riding, but I liked wearing the riding habits for walking. I put on a matching green hat with a wide bow that tied under my chin.

Hector, as always, had breakfast ready. Since I was the first one up, I ate alone, drinking fresh well water. I couldn't stand the taste of coffee, so water was pretty much the only thing I ever drank.

"Headed out to the lake to do some painting?" Hector asked.

"Yes," I said, smiling at him. "But don't tell anyone, okay?"

"Your secret is safe with me, Miss Bailey."

I knew that he would tell someone if I didn't come back by lunchtime. And I knew that he knew that I meant I did not want any of my beaus tagging along.

Living in the house, Hector knew everything that went on. Fortunately, he was very discrete and trustworthy.

He packed me a snack without me even having to ask.

"Be careful out there," he said. "You have your weapon?"

"I always keep it with me," I said.

"Good girl."

I brought my charcoals and sketchbook today. Not because I didn't want to paint, but because it was the first time I had been up to Bierstadt since I had seen the man watching me.

Bringing my paints and supplies was more than I wanted to carry right now. I needed to make sure I felt safe before I lugged all that out there again.

The morning was cool and I was thankful I had on my long-sleeved dress. Although it promised to be a beautiful spring day, it was still cold this morning.

I had second thoughts as I stepped out the back door. It would be so much more pleasant to just sit in front of the fireplace and sketch from memory.

But I wanted—needed—to get back out there. To prove to myself that I was not insane.

And if the man was really there, I wanted to see him more closely.

Out of the corner of my eyes, he had looked quite handsome and I had to admit that I had been thinking about him.

I also had to admit that thinking about a man who wasn't really there had me concerned about my own sanity.

So off I went. My steps falling quietly on the soft dirt trail. Chipmunks darting left and right. Getting as close as they dared before running off as I walked past them.

The birds were in the midst of their morning song to welcome the day, making the morning seem bright and peaceful.

I loved the way the birds cheerfully welcomed each day, seeming to celebrate them even. So much different from humans who often groaned and bellyached about having to get up in the mornings.

Walking through the forest, fragrant with fir and spruce trees, I told myself not to be nervous.

I had mostly managed to convince myself that the man had simply been a mirage.

I had learned about mirages as we traveled across the desert to get here.

Had even seen one myself.

So I knew I was not immune.

And the whole experience made me think.

Maybe even though I denied that I wanted a husband, well… perhaps I really did.

Steeling myself, I went back to the same spot where I had sat painting the last time I was here, but the grass was too damp to sit on.

Instead I went to a boulder at the edge of the lake and sat. It wasn't the most level of rocks, but I good balance and once I sat down, I was fine. The sun was warm on my skin. I left my hat on, though, because I knew from experience that the deceptively pleasant sun could cause a girl some pretty severe sunburn.

I took out my sketchbook, turned to a fresh page, and looked around for something to sketch. The tall mountains and trees near the lake perfectly reflected in the clear sparkling water.

Now I was wishing I had brought my paints. I'd do a sketch and paint it later from memory as best I could. Every time I came up here, the view was a little bit different.

In spite of the beauty and tranquility surrounding me, I still had that nervous feeling.

Reaching into my bag, I pulled out my little gun.

Before we came west, even during the war, I never ever would have thought that I would be one of those women who carried a gun.

But now that I lived out here in the wild west, things had changed. It was actually Drake who had given me the gun. Told me to keep it with me at all times.

My family knew about it and not a single one of them disagreed with Drake. They knew that I liked to go off by myself to paint and sketch.

So I carried it, but this was the first day I had taken it out of my bag other than the day Drake had shown me how to use it.

I laid it on the rock beside me and picked up my charcoal pencil.

Then I caught sight of an elk at the edge of the lake. I barely breathed as it stood perfectly still, its ears twitching. It must have decided I was no danger, because it stayed, bending gracefully to drink from the clear water of the lake.

I began sketching, capturing the graceful lines of the beautiful animal. The little ripples that flowed out from his drinking. I could fill in the background later.

But I quickly lost myself in my work and forgot that I was supposed to be wary of mirages.

CHAPTER 7
GRAHAM

$\mathcal{A}$s a park ranger, I had certain duties. Even on my days off.

The rain stopped as quickly as it had begun. For an afternoon shower, it was quite pleasant.

I stepped out from beneath the trees and walked back toward the lake. I wasn't ready to leave yet.

I stood at the edge of the lake and wondered if maybe there was some kind of eclipse today that I wasn't aware of. I'd had my head stuck in the sand for the last few days, trying to get past today, so it could be.

Something looked different. It looked like early morning instead of early afternoon.

I tried to convince myself that I was being fanciful.

The weather up here in the mountains was unpredictable at best and since the sun was hidden behind the clouds, there was really no way to tell what time it was. Despite the clouds obscuring the sun, the mountains and trees were perfectly reflected in the lake. The greens and blues made a perfect picture. I took out my camera and took a few pictures.

I turned around in a circle and when I turned back, I saw her.

The girl was sitting about six feet away from me. She sat on a boulder much like the one I stood on.

Today she wore a long emerald green dress. Like before, the skirt billowed out around her like she was sitting in the middle of a lily pad. A princess sitting on a lily pad. As far as ghosts from the past went, this one was lovely.

Her long brunette hair flowed around her. She appeared to have made the effort to pull it back, tying it in a loose bow, but it didn't stop it from framing her face.

Her eyes were intent on sketching something. I followed her gaze to see an elk standing perfectly still, his head high, sniffing the air.

I think he must have caught my scent, because he turned and dashed into the trees.

The girl turned and looked directly at me.

"You," she said softly.

When I didn't answer, she tucked a strand of hair behind an ear. "You frightened my elk."

"I'm sorry," I said. "I didn't see him in time."

That put a frown on the lily pad princess's face. She looked down at her sketchpad. "It's okay," she said.

I took a step closer. The only way for me to get to the boulder she was sitting on was to step off mine, walk around, and step onto hers.

I didn't want to let her out of my sight for that long for fear that she would vanish again.

"What are you doing here?" I asked.

"Sketching," she said, wiping her hands on a white cloth.

"Can I see?" I asked.

She shifted, seemed to consider my request, and that's when I saw the glint of steel.

"You can't have that in the park," I said, reflexively.

"Have what? A sketchpad?"

"That." I nodded pointedly. "The gun."

"Oh." With one hand still on her sketchpad, she lowered her other hand to the gun. "Why not?"

I didn't even have my own weapon, so if she had been a threat, which I was certain she was not, I would have been defenseless.

"It's against regulations."

Closing her sketchpad, she seemed to decide not to show me her drawing. "It's for protection," she said.

"I understand," I said.

"I have to go," she stuffed her pad of paper and her pencil into her bag.

"Wait," I said. "Don't go."

She picked up the little pistol and slid it into her bag.

"I have to get home."

"Can I walk you home?" I asked. "I'm a park ranger," I added quickly.

"I don't know you. So no."

As she went to stand, I stood perfectly still.

"I think we got off on the wrong foot," I said. "My name is Graham."

She almost smiled. I saw the corners of her lips lift, but then she seemed to change her mind.

As she reached down to pick up her bag, she lost her balance.

And although she made a valiant effort to right herself, she quite simply fell off the rock into the water.

I knew the water wasn't deep here, but it was rocky and it was cold.

Without the least bit of hesitation, I jumped off my rock to catch her.

She came up sputtering by the time I reached her.

Since the water was shallow enough that I was standing, I

helped her stand as well.

She grabbed my arms as she steadied herself and looked into my eyes.

Her eyes were stunningly green. The emerald green of her now soaked dress paled in comparison to the emerald green of her eyes.

And her eyes weren't just a beautiful color. They held a depth that a man could easily fall into and get lost in.

She looked at me with an odd mix of knowledge and depth.

I had the sensation that I knew her. Yet I knew I had never seen her before.

"Are you okay?" I asked. "Did you hit your head?"

"No," she said. "I'm not injured. But…"

"But?"

"My dress is ruined. And…" She untied her hat and swept it off her head. "My hat."

"It'll dry," I said, although I really didn't know if it would dry properly or not.

The only salient thought I had right now was that I now knew that this girl was not a ghost.

The last I had heard, a man could not touch a ghost.

And I was more than certain that ghosts did not have green eyes.

If they did, someone would have surely said so.

CHAPTER 8
BAILEY

The man was nothing other than a perfect gentleman.

Yet, still, there was something about him that I found unsettling.

It could be the way he had suddenly appeared. I had been happily sketching an elk, doing a decent job of adding in his reflection in the water when this man had suddenly appeared, frightening off my elk.

That in itself had me feeling cross.

But then I had gone and lost my balance. That was his fault, too, although I hadn't quite figured out how.

To his credit, he was in the water at my side before I even came up for air.

So here we were standing in freezing water and neither one of us seemed inclined to move.

I found it most disconcerting.

But even more disconcerting was that I was certain he was the man I had seen earlier. That I could see only from the corner of my eye.

I looked directly at him now, my hands on his arms. His eyes were a lovely aquamarine blue. But they were haunted.

There was a pain behind them that my artist's eyes saw immediately.

I saw a mixture of pain and kindness swirling together in his handsome face.

I had immediately trusted him, but at the same time he frightened me. There was something different about him.

He wasn't a man like Charlie, or Drake, or even Thomas who could be swayed with a smile and a bat of the eyelashes.

This man reminded me of someone, but right at this moment, standing in the freezing water, my wet dress wrapped around my legs, I couldn't think.

My brain had in effect shut down. It could be the cold. It could be the way he was looking at me.

Maybe a little of both.

Whatever it was, I knew that I needed to get out of this freezing water. To get home and warm before I caught my death of cold.

"Let me help you," he said, taking my hand and leading me toward the bank.

I held onto his hand for dear life. I did not know how to swim and being in the water quite frankly terrified me.

My foot slipped on a little rock on the lake floor and I grabbed hold of him, with both hands now.

He reached down and scooped me up in his arms. Carried me easily to the bank and set me on my feet.

"Don't move," he said, after we were standing safely on the bank. "I'll get your things."

While he was gone, I did my best to discretely wring some of the water out of my skirts, at least enough that I could walk. But less than a minute later he was back with my bag over his shoulder

"Where are you parked?" he asked.

Such a strange question. Perhaps I had hit my head after all. It was probably just the cold though.

"My house is over there." Shivering, I held up a hand and pointed.

"Okay," he said. "Let's get you home."

Unable to do much else, I let him take my hand again.

Although I felt unsettled, I really didn't mind holding his hand. I tried not to think about my tumble into the lake. If he hadn't been there…

No, I corrected myself. If he hadn't been there, I would not have rushed to gather up my things to get away from him.

What is it, though, that had my nerves on edge around him?

I looked at him out of the corner of my eyes.

Then I realized just who he reminded me of.

He reminded me of my older sister Andrea's husband, Reed.

It was something in the way he walked. Something in the way he moved. The way he dressed.

Maybe it was his boldness.

And although we never talked about it. I knew. We all knew.

Reed was from the future.

CHAPTER 9
GRAHAM

It only took us fifteen minutes to get to the girl's house from the lake. For all intents and purposes, she lived on Bierstadt Lake. In the national park.

Whiskey Springs was just outside the park and the only people who actually lived inside the park were me and the other ranger.

And, it seemed, this family.

The house was a large two story with a back porch running the length of it. The second-floor balcony also ran the length.

The house had the flavor a southern plantation house, but just a flavor. It was much too plain and rugged to pull that off. No Greek columns. No French windows.

It was well kept though. The paint was fresh and the railings were sturdy.

The minute we walked through the back door, everything moved into what to me seemed like controlled chaos.

A small Chinese man by the name of Hector insisted that I use the guest room upstairs to change into dry clothes that he brought me.

He ignored my insistance that I would be fine. That I could

make it home. That my clothes would dry quickly in the dry air.

"You save Miss Bailey's life," he said. "You must stay for supper." And with that, he was gone.

Bailey. So that was my lily pad princess's name. A beautiful name for a beautiful girl.

One of Bailey's sisters had swept her off to her own room to get her out of her soaked dress and into something dry.

I locked the door and took my time changing my clothes. The pants were baggy—old fashioned, but they fit well enough, considering they were a couple inches too short. The white button-down cotton shirt fit me also. The boots he gave me were a little small, but I could wear them. I tucked the pants in them to hide their shortness.

I had managed to lose my ball cap somewhere, most likely when I slid into the lake, so I just brushed my already dry hair.

I laid my wet blue jeans across a wooden chair. They would be dry soon enough.

After I was dressed, I took some time to look around. The room was sparse except for a full-size four-poster bed draped with mosquito netting and a little dresser.

A lovely painting of Longs Peaks with a sky in purples and blues that surely had to come from the artist's imagination.

If the room had a writing desk, I mused, it would be the perfect guest room.

With nothing else to do, I left the room and headed for the stairs.

When I reached the landing, I stopped.

The grandfather clock at the bottom of the stairs began to chime the hour. I waited and counted. It was only ten o'clock in the morning.

Surely the clock must be wrong. Then I remembered how it seemed like it was earlier in the day than I thought.

Everything about today was bizarre. There was nothing I could do about it. I could only go with it.

I would happily take bizarre over what had happened one year ago today. More than happily. I was glad to have the distraction.

And now I could find out exactly who Bailey was.

Besides just the lily pad princess of my imagination.

CHAPTER 10
BAILEY

"*I* knew something bad was going to happen to you going off by yourself like that," Dakota said as she came back from taking my soaked dress out to the balcony to dry.

"It wasn't that bad," I said.

"Oh," she said, holding up my ruined emerald green hat. "Are you sure you're my sister? Looks like your new hat is ruined."

I just shrugged. "I'll get another one."

Dakota scowled at me. "Yesterday, this was your favorite hat."

"I did like it," I said, looking at the crumpled lump of velvet that had indeed been my favorite hat.

I would have ordinarily been saddened about it, but at the moment I had something entirely more interesting on in my mind.

Giving up on figuring me out, Dakota sat next to me on the bed and took the hairbrush from my hand.

"You have such long, wayward hair," she said.

"No one seems to mind," I said, closing my eyes to relax for just a moment. By no one, I meant the men who came courting.

"Are you going to tell me your secret to getting men to follow you home, no matter where you go?"

I laughed. "Very funny. He was merely escorting me home after making me fall in the lake."

Dakota's hands stilled in my hair. "He pushed you into the water?"

"No," I said. "but it was his fault nonetheless."

Dakota continued to brush my hair, a little smile on her lips.

"What's funny?" I asked.

"You," she said. "And your men. I guess you've got a fourth one who will be hanging around now."

"They aren't my men," I said. But her statement made me cringe a little bit.

There was something different about Graham. Something I would like to explore further.

And I didn't know for sure, but I had a feeling he might not be the kind of guy to hang around if there were other men vying for my attention.

"He's staying for supper?" I asked.

"Of course," Dakota said. "You don't think Hector would let him leave after he saved your life."

"It was his fault to begin with," I said, channeling my nervousness into feeling cross.

"Well," Dakota said. "He's kinda good looking."

"I guess you could say that," I agreed with a little shrug.

But Dakota was grinning.

Unable to keep quiet any longer, I turned and looked straight at my sister.

"Does he remind you of Reed?" I asked. "Even a little bit?"

"Andrea's husband Reed?"

"Yes," I said. "Andrea's husband Reed."

Dakota seemed to consider. "Maybe a little I guess." She frowned. "How?"

"The way he was dressed. The way he moves."

"I guess I didn't look at him that close."

I left it alone. Dakota didn't see it, but I did.

And I knew.

A man like Graham didn't just appear out of nowhere like that.

CHAPTER 11
GRAHAM

When I'd gotten out of bed this morning, I never would have thought I would be having dinner with the Auclair family tonight.

I sat next to Colton, across from Bailey. Her other two sisters, Dakota and Elise sat at the other end of the table.

All three of the girls wore long dresses and looked like they had stepped out of the past.

Colton was dressed like me. Pants and white shirt.

"We should play parlor games after supper," Elise, the youngest one said as Hector brought out plates filled with mashed potatoes, corn, and peas.

Bailey glanced over to see my reaction. I just smiled at her. She smiled back and demurely lowered her lashes.

"I'm sure Graham has other things to do besides stay here and play games with us," Dakota said.

Oddly enough, Colton was the one who jumped to my defense. "You can't just send him home after dark. He'll stay in the guest room."

All three sisters just looked at him.

"What?" he asked. "That's what it's there for."

"It's Andrea's room," Elise said.

"And Andrea lives in Denver now," Colton said. "With her husband."

"I don't want to be an inconvenience," I said. And I certainly didn't want to be in the middle of a family argument.

"They argue about everything," Bailey said. "He's right though. It's already too dark to travel."

"Especially tonight," Colton added. "It's a new moon, so you won't be able to see a thing. Unless you live across the street, it won't be safe. You could find yourself walking off the side of a mountain."

"Do you live in Whiskey Springs?" Dakota asked.

"No," I said. "I live in the park."

They were all looking at me now as though I had sudden started speaking a foreign language.

"What park?" Elise asked.

"The Rocky Mountain National Park," I said. Maybe these people had somehow isolated themselves from the world.

"I told you," Bailey said, looking pointedly at Dakota.

"Doesn't mean anything," Dakota said.

"It could," Bailey said, then turned back and smiled sweetly at me.

"You have to stay the night," she said.

She was like a siren pulling me toward the dangerous rocks. And I couldn't resist her.

Even worse, I didn't want to.

I wanted to fall into her eyes and stay there forever.

"You sound like you're from back East," Dakota said.

"I am," I said. "I'm from—" Pittsburgh.

But I couldn't say it out loud.

Everything I had tamped down all day came back to me in a rush.

All the images. All the feelings.

I thought I had everything under control.

"I'm sorry," I said. I think I said it out loud. My ears were ringing and I felt like I was going to pass out right here.

Bailey came around the table and everything was hazy after that.

CHAPTER 12
BAILEY

Shooing my siblings away, I led Graham out back. Hector handed me a couple of warm cloaks on our way out the door.

The air was cold and Colton was right. It was already dark and the moon wasn't coming out tonight.

The rushing sounds of the river traveling on the cold air tangled itself with the music from the saloon across the street. A wolf howled somewhere, then there was nothing but the roar of the river and music.

As far as saloons went, it seemed tame enough. Not that I had any experience in that area other than what I had read and what people had told me. People mostly being Thomas. He spent some time there drinking and gambling and didn't mind talking about it.

I hadn't known Graham very long, but I recognized that he needed some air and needed some space to get through whatever it was he was experiencing.

He certainly didn't need everyone staring at him.

I had never told anyone, but I sometimes felt like my world was ending when people talked about our parents.

No one knew that my ears would ring and I would feel like I was going to pass out right then and there.

I'd learned to sit quietly until it passed, then hide it behind a flirty smile and a bat of my eyelashes.

I led him to the swing at the end of the porch and sitting next to him, gently rocked the swing.

It seemed to help. He took a deep breath and looked over at me in the darkness, a soft glow from the window the only light.

"Sorry about that," he said.

"You don't have to apologize," I said. "My family can be a bit overwhelming at times."

"It wasn't them," he said. "It was just…"

"It's okay," I said, putting a hand over his. "You don't have to talk about it."

He nodded and looked away into the darkness.

"I didn't know this was here," he said.

"It's a little town," I said. "Not much to it."

He turned and looked at me again, his face merely a shadowy outline. "Whiskey Springs," he said.

He turned his hand over, our palms touching now, sending little tingles up and down my spine and making my heart speed up. I wondered if he could feel my blood pumping.

"The main part of the town is down the hill," I said. "This is just what I would call a village. We have a few houses, including Dr. Avery's, a saloon, and a café. The rest of the town is down a little ways. On the other side of the river."

I was telling him all these things I was certain he already knew on purpose in an effort to distract him from whatever demons troubled him.

"I see," he said.

"You'll stay?" I asked, suddenly realizing that I wanted him to stay. Very much.

"I don't think I have a choice," he said with a little laugh.

"You have family here?" I asked.

He was quiet again. And I didn't think he was going to answer me. I realized too late that I had stepped back into whatever it was he was trying to avoid.

"I don't have any family," he said. "In fact, it happened one year ago today."

I linked my fingers with his. "I'm so sorry," I said and even though I didn't know what it was I was sorry about, I meant it. I hated seeing him in pain.

CHAPTER 13
GRAHAM

The Auclair siblings had apparently gone ahead with their parlor games without us. Their voices and occasional laughter drifted outside.

The festive music from a saloon provided background noise.

The scent of wood smoke reminded me of the campgrounds in the park.

They had no electricity and although I wanted to ask, it didn't seem right to do so. The odd thing was I hadn't seen any light fixtures.

I was content to sit here in the darkness and relative quietness with Bailey, my lily pad princess. She wasn't wearing green now. She was wearing a light blue dress, but still a princess.

"My family is… was… from Pittsburgh," I said.

She sat very quietly, waiting, not saying anything.

I'd never talked to anyone about this. I hadn't had to. Everyone just knew. Even my therapist had known. Probably not the best therapist since she had let me get away with not saying what had happened out loud.

I didn't blame her though. It had been horrendous and unthinkable. Something no one should have to go through.

"I was the only one who survived." There. I had said the words out loud to another human being. I couldn't explain why Bailey was the person I chose to tell, but there it was.

"They hadn't been sure I was going to survive either for awhile." From what they told me, it had been touch and go for a few days.

What they didn't know, was that there had been days after that, after I learned what happened, that I did not want to live. Only my therapist knew that. Sort of.

After all, there was no one else to tell. I certainly wasn't going to go around telling people I didn't know. Certainly not even classmates or professors. They, in fact, lauded me for my survival.

"I don't—"

Before Bailey could say whatever she was going to say, the back door burst open and Elise swirled out the door, bringing a burst of light with her.

"Come on," she said. "We need you to play musical chairs."

I looked at Bailey. "Is she serious?" I asked.

"I'm afraid so," she said. "Do you mind terribly?

"I don't mind."

The last time I remembered playing musical chairs, I was in kindergarten. But, it seems, I had been missing out.

These people didn't seem bothered by not having Internet or electricity. And from the looks of it, they had far more fun than anybody could have playing video games or watching television.

They had pushed the sofa back against the wall and arranged four wooden chairs in the middle of the floor, back to back.

Colton was the designated music person.

We all lined up in front of the chairs.

Colton turned his back to us and started playing a harmonica. Very badly.

"We all have a chair," I said to Bailey, walking in front of me.

"It won't last long," she said.

The music stopped and we all took a chair.

Colton turned and grinning, removed one of the chairs. "That was the easy part."

Then Colton continued to play the harmonica as I walked around the chairs with the three sisters.

I was about to get dizzy when he stopped. Everyone grabbed a chair, but Elise was left standing without one.

"Mon Dieu," she said, but she was laughing.

They removed another chair.

This time Dakota was left standing.

Now we were down to one chair. It was just me and Bailey now.

With Colton playing, a generous description, his harmonica, Bailey and I circled the single chair, with only candlelight to guide us.

I locked my gaze on hers as we circled. She smiled impishly at me from beneath her lashes as we went round and round. Sometimes moving slowly, sometimes speeding up.

Colton stopped.

We both stood on either side of the chair.

I sat first, but as she went for the chair, my arms went around her and she ended up in my lap.

We were both laughing.

Dakota and Elise clapped.

The clock began to chime the hour.

With our arms around each other, we gazed at one another until the clock went back to its regular steady ticking.

It occurred to me that this was the most fun I had had since that day. One year ago today.

I never would have expected it. Not in a million years.
And the irony was unthinkable.

CHAPTER 14
BAILEY

*I*t was late when we all went to our rooms.

I changed into my nightgown, but soon discovered that I was unable to sleep.

Tossing and turning, I stared up at the dark ceiling above. I kept thinking about Graham. Wondering if he was okay. Wondering what had happened to him. Replaying the way it had felt to be in his arms when I had accidentally sat down in his lap.

Giving up on sleep, I pulled on my warm cloak and went downstairs, drawn to the warmth of the fireplace.

Since no one else was downstairs, I curled up on the sofa, my feet beneath me and watched the red and gold flames of the fire.

Graham had been a good sport, playing along with us, but I was worried about him.

Something had happened to his family back in Pittsburgh a year ago. I think he was about to tell me about it, but Elise had interrupted.

It was probably a good thing. No one need to relive something that caused a person to lose their entire family.

In my experience, talking about such things did not make them better. The only thing that made them better was time. Time and not being reminded of it.

That's how it was for me anyway. I didn't want to talk about the day the letter had come telling us about our father or the day we were called to our mother's bedside to say goodbye. Those were days I wanted to purge from my mind. To never think about again.

That was one of the reasons I liked it that my sisters and brother and I had moved out here. At the time, I hadn't realized it and hadn't really wanted to go west.

But once we got here, it felt like a new beginning. The constant reminders of painful things were no longer there. And the landscape was stunningly beautiful. I could live here my whole life and never be able to paint all the beautiful things. The elk. The chipmunks. The birds.

Not to mention the mountains.

And there was no stifling, muggy heat like there had been in Mississippi.

The only thing missing was the shopping, but I was becoming accustomed to that. The good outweighed the bad a hundred times over.

And besides my family, I had friends. Drake, Thomas, and Charlie. All three of them wanted to be more, but I didn't. There had never been a romantic pull to any of them.

But now that I had met Graham, things were different. I felt a romantic pull towards him. I knew nothing about him, really, other than that he was a tortured soul like I was.

That and he had the most beautiful blue eyes. Like the sky on a clear spring day.

And beneath the sadness that tortured him, I saw warmth and kindness.

With the warmth of the fire in front of me, I fell asleep thinking about Graham.

Sometime in the night, I woke—or maybe I was dreaming—and saw Graham standing there in front of the fireplace looking at me.

I smiled at him and he smiled back. Then, feeling safe and content, I fell back asleep again, dreaming about him.

When dawn came and I woke with the morning sun streaming in through the window, I was alone.

I hadn't intended to sleep down here on the sofa, but I had slept surprisingly well. Better than I had slept in quite some time.

Sitting up, I stretched. I wasn't the first one up, though. I heard voices coming from the kitchen. Both male and female voices.

Not wanting to be caught sleeping down here on the sofa, especially by Graham, I got up, straightened my nightgown and cloak, then quickly rushed toward the stairs before I could be seen. As I walked past, the grandfather clock began chiming the hour. It was early yet. Only six o'clock. My family rarely got up this early so it was odd that I heard them in the kitchen.

I needed to put on some decent clothes and brush my hair.

Just reaching the top of the stairs, feeling home free, I looked up to see Graham standing there.

"Good morning," he said.

"Good morning," I said, forcing a smile and fighting the instinctual urge to dart back down the stairs.

He held out a hand.

"Did you sleep well?" he asked with a little smile playing about the corners of his lips.

"I 'um." I put my hand in his and my thoughts scattered. "Yes."

"It's much warmer down in front of the fire," he said.

"Yes," I said. "It is much warmer." That's when I remembered waking in the night and seeing him standing in front of the fireplace. But it had only been a dream.

Just a dream.

"Have you had breakfast yet?" he asked.

"Not yet," I said. "I was just coming up to get dressed.

He grinned.

"I'll wait for you then," he said. "Will you have breakfast with me?"

"Of course," I said. "I'll be back after I get dressed."

Still holding my hand, he pulled me toward him.

He bent his head and pressed his lips to mine in a chaste kiss that caused my blood to pound dangerously through my veins. The chaste kiss began to feel a little less chaste as the seconds ticked past.

Then he pulled back and gazed into my eyes. I fell into those sky blue eyes and knew I was lost forever.

Then we both turned, our hands still linked until our fingers slowly slid apart.

I hurried to my room, closing the door, and leaning against the cool wood until my heart rate slowed back to normal.

This man, Graham, made my hands tremble and my heart flutter.

I flirted and played with men, but this was the first time I had ever felt like this.

This was something else entirely.

CHAPTER 15
GRAHAM

*W*hile I waited for Bailey to come downstairs for breakfast, I stepped outside to look around.

It was chilly and although I needed my sweatshirt, I didn't want to go back upstairs for it. My jeans and shirt had dried, so I wore them instead of the clothes I had borrowed last night. It was definitely good to have my own clothes back on.

I walked around to the front of the house and it was just as Bailey had said. Besides this house and a couple of others, there was a saloon, quiet now, and a café, closed.

It all looked new, but old. In fact, I could smell the scent of freshly cut lumber. A wagon rumbled past, the driver an unshaven rugged looking fellow of indeterminate age.

"Howdy," he said, tipping his hat.

"Good morning," I said.

Where had this place come from? Some kind of commune?

This was not part of the park. I was certain of it.

Maybe it was the ghost town.

Feeling edgy and not ready to go back inside, I wandered down the path that led to Bierstadt Lake. It had only taken us a few minutes to get here.

And it only took me a few minutes to get back.

Baffled, I walked to the edge of the water and looked down at my reflection in the perfectly clear water.

"Excuse me," an older man asked, coming up behind me.

I turned, sliding into my role as a park ranger. "Good morning. What can I help you with?"

"Morning," he said with a little laugh and glanced up toward the early afternoon sun. "Can you tell me how to get back to Bear Lake from here? My wife and I seem to have gotten turned around."

"Of course," I said, pointing them in the right direction.

As they took off, I looked around. This was Memorial Day weekend and the tourists were out in full force as proof.

In fact… I was supposed to be at work today.

Startled that I had forgotten, I stood frozen, contemplating what I should do.

I needed to get home. Put on my uniform. Get back out here. I didn't even know where I was assigned today.

I was going to be written up for sure. Not the best way to start off a new job.

And yet. I was pulled back toward Bailey. I'd promised to have breakfast with her.

I would just go back, tell her that I had to go to work and set up a time to come back.

Satisfied that that was my best option, I jogged back down the path that led to her home.

First of all, I was jogging. Second… I stopped. It was taking far longer to get back to the Auclair house than it should have.

I turned around and retraced my steps. Taking my time, now, to look around.

Something beneath a fir tree caught my attention that I hadn't noticed a minute ago when I had jogged this way.

With dread, I walked toward what I already knew I was going to find.

A stone wall about three feet high and what was left of a crumbled chimney.

I stood in front of that chimney and turned around, making a full circle.

This was the Auclair house. This was where I had watched Bailey sleep on the sofa in front of the warm fire. This was where the parlor had been. The one where we had played musical chairs, laughing like children.

Feeling weak in my knees, I sat down on a fallen log.

This was the ghost town.

This was the Auclair house.

It could not be both.

But I was certain I was in the right place.

There were only a limited number of explanations.

I ticked them off in my head.

The most obvious was that the Auclairs were ghosts. But that went against everything I thought I knew.

Second, I was having a psychotic break. This was entirely possible since the day I had spent with people who should not be real was also the anniversary of the tragedy that had struck my family.

I contemplated that for a bit, not having the energy to fight the memories that insisted on filling my thoughts.

It had been a clear spring day almost tipping over into summer.

My family was all there. My parents. My older brother. My younger sister.

My fiancé and her parents.

The pilot had been my only uncle.

This was going to be the adventure of a lifetime. A day we would never forget.

It had not occurred to me or, as far as I knew, anyone in my family that we should not all fly together.

But it was a short flight to Mackinac Island. A destination wedding, they called it.

Mackenzie and I called it a modified elopement.

Instead, it had been a nightmare.

CHAPTER 16
BAILEY

I had taken my time getting ready for breakfast. I'd put on a pale yellow dress, then looked in the mirror, changed my mind, and put on a pretty burgundy one.

I'd taken my time on my hair. Wove a white ribbon through it and tied it at the back.

By the time I got downstairs to the kitchen, everyone else was finished with breakfast.

They were all in the parlor. Elise reading a book. Dakota working on some needlepoint. Colton sitting in the little study off the main room, doing something with ledgers. After our older sister, Andrea, had married and moved to Denver, Colton had taken over the household finances.

I didn't see Graham anywhere.

"Would you like some breakfast, Miss Bailey?" Hector asked, seeing me standing in the kitchen.

"Have you seen Graham?" I asked, taking a glass of water from him.

"Mr. Graham went outside," he said. "I don't think he has come back yet."

"Did he have breakfast?" I asked, the feeling of dread intensifying.

"He didn't have breakfast. He was waiting for you to come down."

I set the glass down and whirled around, going back into the parlor.

"Have you seen Graham?" I asked, going up to Dakota and Elise.

They looked at each other and shook their heads.

"Maybe he went back up to his room," I said.

I took the stairs, did a cursory knock on the guest room door, then opened it.

The bed was made and the clothes he had borrowed were folded neatly on the dresser.

The only thing I saw of his—the only thing indicating that he had even been here—was his jacket.

Picking it up, I held it close. It smelled like him. Like a forest after a rain with a touch of leather.

There was something heavy in the pocket.

I pulled it out and turned it this way and that. It looked like some kind of mirror with dark glass.

Dakota came into the room.

"What's this?" I asked, holding it up for her to see.

She took one look at it. "I don't know, but Reed had one like it."

Reed.

"I told you so," I said, sitting down hard on the bed.

Reed, my sister Andrea's husband, had been from the future. And he had one of these mirrors.

"What does it mean though?" Dakota asked.

I looked at Dakota, my heart in my throat. "It can only mean one thing," I said.

Dakota's eyes widened.

She remembered that day as well as I did.

The day Reed had vanished.

"He's like Reed," I said.

Dakota smiled sadly at me.

"And you're like Andrea."

I didn't want to be.

I just wanted to be a normal girl who someday married a normal man to live a normal life.

But instead, I was in love with a man from the future.

Not exactly normal.

CHAPTER 17
GRAHAM

I moved through the next week in a daze.

I donned my uniform every day. I answered questions. Even led a group of tourists on a guided tour around Bear Lake.

But if anyone had looked at me. Really looked at me. They would have seen that there was no light in my eyes.

I was wrought with guilt.

I had dared to look at another woman other than Mackenzie. And not only had I looked at another woman, I had done it on the one year anniversary of the crash that had taken Mackenzie away from me. Had taken my whole family away from me.

I was a horrible, despicable person.

It would probably have been a good time to call my therapist. A good time to do a sanity check.

But I could not bring myself to do it. I just existed. Letting one day slide into the next.

When I woke the next Saturday morning, I rolled over to see a blue bird sitting on my window ledge looking at me with one eye. I had slept with the window open, so the blue bird could have come inside if he had wanted to. Instead, he just sat there, looking at me.

As I lay there being assessed by a blue bird, it occurred to me that time did not move in a linear fashion.

Time was fluid.

Time was malleable.

Time was everything.

I sat up and the blue bird fluttered off. I suppose his job was done.

It was my day off, so I took my coffee and went out to sit on the front porch. The one that overlooked the moraine.

Early morning mist hovered around the steep mountain peaks, suggesting that a late season snow might be in store. The tourists would love it, I mused.

There was one thing I had to do today. And then, depending on the outcome of that thing, I was going to call my therapist. See about getting some medication.

I felt antsy. That was the only way to describe it.

I hadn't decided which was worse. Feeling antsy or walking around in a daze. The jury was still out.

I took a quick shower, got dressed, and drove into Whiskey Springs.

I parked near the entrance and went inside the library.

"Come with me, Graham."

I followed a woman who seemed to have been waiting for me the moment I stepped through the door.

She didn't exactly look like a librarian. She wore a pencil skirt with a little matching jacket in powder blue, Jackie Kennedy style. Her hair fell onto her shoulders in loose waves. The woman had a classic look to her. She could have blended in anywhere. From here to New York. Probably a little overdressed for Whiskey Springs, but no one seemed to notice, much less mind.

We were halfway across the library floor before I remembered that I wasn't wearing my uniform with my name tag.

I followed her into a cute little alcove set up with a table and chairs and a little window seat. The sign over the window identified it as the "Whiskey Springs" section. One full shelf was full of books. The other wall held a single painting. It was a beautiful blue flower with a lavender, stormy sky behind it. The title on a label below it was *Lavender Blue Number Two.*

The woman took a book from one of the shelves and laid in the table.

"You'll find what you're looking for in here," she said, tapping a well-manicured finger on the narrow, oversized book.

"Thank you," I said, picking up the book. *A Pictorial History of Whiskey Springs.*

I turned to find out how she knew my name and how she knew what I was looking for, but she was gone.

So I just sat down and opened the book.

Ten minutes later, I sat back and stared at the full page photograph.

The entire Auclair family was there. Dakota. Elise. Colton.
And Bailey.

Bailey was wearing a long dress that looked like her emerald green one. The one with the matching hat. The very same hat that had been ruined when she fell into the lake.

I leaned closer, taking in every detail.

It was most definitely her. Down to her bow shaped lips curved in a seductive smile to her eyes that seemed to twinkle even in the black and white photograph.

According to the text, the other couple in the photograph was their sister Andrea and her husband, Reed Smith.

I looked over my shoulder for the librarian, but didn't see her anywhere.

Moving past the photograph, I read that the Auclairs had lived in a part of Whiskey Springs that was now part of Rocky Mountain National Park.

So I was right. They lived in the ghost town. Village. Whatever.

But Bailey had said that Whiskey Springs was just across the river. I didn't understand that.

Just as I slid the book back onto the shelf, the librarian appeared by my side again.

I jumped.

"Are things making sense to you now?" she asked.

"Not really, no."

"Sit," she said.

I did as she asked, sitting across from her.

She clasped her hands together in front of her and searched my gaze.

"I have something to tell you," she said. "Something that you might not want to hear."

"Something to do with Bailey Auclair?" I asked.

"In a way, yes," she said. "But that's not the part that you won't want to hear."

I sat back, crossed my arms.

The last year of my life had been full of things I had not wanted to hear. As far as I was concerned things could not get any worse for me.

Nonetheless, I felt my eyes glazing over with their protective shield.

"I'm listening," I said.

"Graham," she said. "I am your great great great... maybe another great... aunt."

"I see."

Either I wasn't the only one out of touch with reality or she was part of my psychotic orbit.

"Did your mother ever tell you a story about Vaughn Becquerel?"

She was asking me to think back on one of those memories that should have been happy, but instead was shadowed by the bad.

"Maybe in the guise of a bedtime story about a young girl who traveled to America from France in the 1700s," she suggested.

"The Indians killed everyone but her," I said.

"That's right. Do you remember how they saved her life?"

My sister had been more interested in this particular fairy tale, but she wasn't here to answer these questions. It was just me.

"Graham," the woman said. "You survived for a reason."

"No," I said. "You can't know this." I pushed back my chair and went to stand up.

"Graham," she gently put a hand on my wrist. "Wait. Please hear me out."

Her touch had a calming effect on my system. Or maybe it was her calm voice. Maybe both.

I sat back down.

"Thank you," she said.

"Why?" I asked. "Why did I survive when no one else did?" My voice was strained. Gravelly.

A semblance of a smile twitched at her lips.

"I ask myself that every day. And I'll be honest with you. The answer never comes."

"I don't—"

"You're not going to understand because there is nothing to understand. There is no answer. Not one that we can know."

My eyes misted over as I stared at her and I gripped the edges of the table until my hands ached.

It hardly registered with me that I was shaking my head.

She held out her hand, palm up. I put my hand in hers, my eyes never leaving hers.

"I am Vaughn Becquerel. I was the one who survived by going through time."

"How are you here?" I asked, my voice barely recognizable to my own ears.

"The rip in time never healed." She took a breath. Gave me a second to absorb her words. "With the help of my daughter, a physicist, somehow I sort of control my time travels now. But when someone needs help with their life's purpose, I automatically go to them."

"How do you know… things?"

"That's something I can't answer. Not even for myself."

A car went by outside the window, music blaring. Reminding of where I was.

"I survived," I said. "But I'm still here."

"Remember the great great part…?" She rolled her eyes. "great great great great?"

I almost smiled. "Yes. I remember."

"The spell is weaker now. And you are only distantly related. But somehow it still works."

"You say this like it's a good thing," I said.

She narrowed her eyes and studied me. "I've taken a special interest in you," she said. "You and I are so much alike."

I realized I was shaking my head again. Catching myself, I stopped.

"We both survived the impossible."

"What's the point?" I asked before I caught myself.

"The point is the spell only works to bring people together for love." She took a deep breath. "I didn't know this until much later, but when the old Indian spoke, part of what he said was in Latin, so I didn't understand it."

"An Indian who spoke Latin?"

"Not really an Indian," she said, dismissing the

inconsistency. "It was only later that I learned he had thrown in a love spell."

"Mackenzie," I said with a lump in my throat.

"I know, Dear," she said, squeezing my hand. "I'm hopeful that it will make sense to you later."

I sat back, let my fingers slide from hers as I studied her.

"You are not psychotic," she said.

This woman who claimed to be Vaughn Becquerel seemed to know everything about me. Even things that no one else knew.

I was inclined to believe that she was real.

"Bailey Auclair," I said, nodding in the general direction of the book she had shown me."

"Yes," she said, sitting back herself. "I never tell anyone this, but I had... have... depending on the moment, two great loves in my life. I could not choose one over the other if my life or even their lives depended on it."

"I don't have that choice."

"Exactly," she said. "That's why I believe in this spell. I believe in a higher power. You and I, I suspect will never know. It's not our place to know. It's only our place to do or die. As they say."

I took a deep ragged breath. "Are you sure I'm not psychotic? Because I think you're in my head."

She laughed softly. "Graham Daniels," she said. "You are going to be okay. You're a survivor in every way."

"Still," I said. "I don't understand."

"You're in love with Bailey Auclair?" she asked.

"I just met her."

Vaughn scoffed. "You're a man. A man knows in an instant. Quick," she said. "Don't think. Just answer. Are you in love with her?"

"Yes," I said.

She smiled a deep, mysterious smile. "In that case, I can help you."

I narrowed my eyes at her. "Will I see you again?"

"Not after today," she said. "But you must remember one thing. Tuck it into your heart and let it grow."

"What is that thing?" I asked.

"You survived for a reason."

CHAPTER 18
BAILEY

*I*t was a beautiful summer day in the mountains.

After my encounter with Graham, I had become restless. I understood now why my sister had left here. Why she couldn't stay.

It was impossible not to watch for him at every turn.

Even when I had a paint canvas in front of me, I had trouble keeping my focus on task for very long.

It annoyed me. It saddened me. It warmed my heart.

But where Andrea had left, I had stayed. I did not want to leave here.

Everything I loved was here. The mountains. The clear lakes. The seasons.

So I found a way to channel my excess energy.

I planted a small garden on the north side of the house. It got both evening sun and morning sun, but mostly morning sun.

I jabbed the hoe into the dirt and made a space to toss in half a potato. I had a bucket of potatoes, all cut in half, ready to plant. Come fall, we'd have potatoes.

Not that we needed potatoes. We could get them from the

General Store. But, again, it helped to use up some of my excess energy.

I had to time my gardening just after a rain, though, because the ground was dry by nature. So different from the muggy Mississippi weather.

It had been two weeks since the day Graham had caused me to fall into the lake. I had decided it was his fault because he was too handsome and he had been looking at me in a distracting manner.

So I made myself a garden.

And over the past two weeks I had systematically avoided Drake and Thomas. Charlie was here now, helping me with my garden.

He stopped, leaned on his hoe and looked at me.

"What's wrong?" I asked, feeling cross, not with him in particular. Just cross in general.

"Are you ever going to marry me?"

"What?" I asked, giving my head a quick shake and giving my eyes a hard blink.

"Well," Charlie said. "I noticed that Drake and Thomas haven't been coming around, but you're not paying me much attention either."

"Nonsense," I said, jabbing my hoe in the ground again.

He put a hand on mine to stop me.

"I'm serious," he said.

I'd never seen Charlie like this. He'd always been easy going and undemanding. He'd never even tried to steal a kiss.

It was occurring to me in this moment that maybe I had taken him a little bit for granted.

"Charlie," I said. "What are you talking about?"

"I've been coming over here for a few months now. And I thought we were going to get married."

I forced myself to close my mouth and not gape at him in disbelief.

"This is not something we ever talked about."

He swept a hand over my little garden.

"Didn't think I had to," he said.

"Oh."

I bit my lip and studied him.

Charlie wasn't a bad looking guy. He was average height. Lean. Enough muscles. I'd just never thought of him that way.

Sure. I knew in the back of my mind that he probably wanted to court me, but I honestly didn't have a clear idea of what that looked like.

My sister Andrea had married Reed after knowing him only a short time and he had lived in our home the whole time.

But then Reed was different…

And thinking about Reed brought my thoughts full circle around back to Graham.

I couldn't stop thinking about Graham.

"Never mind," Charlie said, releasing my hand and jabbing his hoe into the ground. "Forget I said anything."

"Charlie," I said.

Charlie turned his back to me and kept working. I had hurt him. I hadn't meant to.

But Graham was the one I thought about when I went to sleep at night and the one I thought about when I woke up in the morning.

Graham had one big problem though.

Graham was from the future.

I had to accept that he may never come back.

"Charlie," I said, sternly. He looked over his shoulder and waited. Listening.

"Are you ever going to ask me properly?"

CHAPTER 19
GRAHAM

I was not an impulsive man.

I'd told Vaughn that I was in love with Bailey. And I had not lied. I didn't lie either.

But what she didn't and couldn't understand was that loving Bailey was eating me alive with guilt.

Mackenzie had died the very day I was going to make her my wife.

How was a man supposed to cope with something like that? How did a thing like that even happen?

And it just didn't sit right with me going from what had happened with Mackenzie to being in love with Bailey.

I put a frozen burrito in the oven and sat down at the table.

I had checked out the library book. I'd checked it out and I wasn't planning on giving it back. I'd almost offered to pay the fine right then and there, but then I'd remembered that I was a national park ranger and it would look bad for me to do a premeditated book theft.

Opening the book, I went to the photograph. I had come home and read the whole book, but I hadn't really learned anything. It was just a general history of Whiskey Springs.

But the photograph was something else entirely.

With a burst of inspiration, I had taken a photo of the picture and zoomed in so I could see them up close.

I quickly affirmed that Colton, Dakota, and Elise were the Auclairs I had met.

Then I zoomed in on Bailey's picture and left it there.

I left her picture on my computer while I ate my burrito.

I left it there while I took a beer out of fridge and popped the top. I rarely drank beer, but tonight it seemed like a good idea to do just that.

After taking no more than a couple of sips of the beer, my land line rang. The older ranger, Maggie, had collapsed right in the middle of giving her campfire program.

They had rushed her to the ER in Whiskey Springs. He wanted me there for support. So I locked up, jumped in my truck, and drove back to Whiskey Springs.

My boss, Leonard, met me at the door.

"How's she doing?" I asked."

"They think it's her heart," he said. "They're running some tests."

"Where's everyone else?" I asked.

"May or may not come," he said, turning around with a vague wave of his hand.

As we walked inside, that distinctive scent of antiseptic hit me like a wave. Memories flooded back of the weeks I had spent cooped up in a hospital bed. Eating bad hospital food. Watching bad television. Grieving.

We sat in the sparsely decorated waiting room where no telling how many people had sat waiting to hear the fate of their loved ones. I had never had the luxury. I had been the one people would have been waiting to hear about except that there was no one to do the waiting.

"Want some coffee?" Leonard asked.

"Sure," I said.

When he came back with two cups of coffee, nasty and black, I took mine and just held it.

It was late and quiet, at least in this part of the hospital. A small town like this, if anything happened, it would light everything up.

I'd expected more people to be here for Maggie. Figured that Leonard had called all of us.

"Why did you call me?" I asked.

Leonard looked over at me. Shrugged.

"I called all of you," he said, meaning all five of us full-time park rangers. "You're the only one who could come."

I sniffed the coffee. Definitely deciding against drinking it.

"What about her family?" I asked. "They couldn't be here?"

Leonard looked at me. Straightened the seam of his pants. He was still wearing his park uniform.

"Maggie doesn't have anyone."

"What do you mean?" His words startled me. There weren't that many people who had absolutely no one. I was an anomaly. My mother was an only child. My father had one brother. No children.

"She's lived in the park for years," he said. "The park is her life. No husband. No kids. All her family of origin is long gone."

I stood up. Walked to the door. Watched the nurses at the nurse's station. Everyone was tapping on computers.

"How old is Maggie?" I asked over my shoulder.

"Fifty-four."

Damn. Maggie was me in about twenty years. Lived alone in the park. No family. None. Only her boss and the new guy showed up at the hospital after she collapsed on the job.

Leonard answered his phone and left me to my own devices. I walked outside and watered the grass with toxic coffee. Tossed the cup in the trash.

It was cold, but the air felt good.

I needed the sting of the fresh air.

I sat on the first park bench I came to and contemplated my day.

After finally pulling myself out of a daze, I had gone to the library and found out that the Auclair family lived in the 1860s. In what was now a ghost town.

Then I had met Vaughn Becquerel. Alive and well. Vaughn was supposed to be a legend. Not a fashionable librarian.

And now this. My coworker's life was in the balance and she had no one there for her.

She was me. I was her.

Mackenzie was gone. There was no bringing her back.

I had pretty much come to terms about that.

I had loved her and a part of me always would.

But living brought responsibilities with it. And one of those responsibilities was to live life to its fullest.

It just so happened that in order for me to live my life to its fullest, I had to go back to the 1860s.

CHAPTER 20
BAILEY

orking out in my little garden had become my routine and this morning had started off no different except for one thing.

Instead of wielding a hoe, I was wielding a paint brush.

I sat on a little wooden stool, my chocolate brown skirts pillowed out around me.

The blooms on a purple wildflower had caught my attention. Fortunately I had seen it before Charlie took a hoe to it. I'd threatened him within an inch of his life if he chopped it down. Neither of us knew what kind of flower it was. I just knew that I wanted to capture it on a paint canvas.

Charlie wasn't here this morning. He had something he needed to do. So I had the unusual opportunity to sit with my own thoughts.

I had somehow come to the conclusion that spending my life waiting for a man who may or may not come back to me— from the future no less—was not in my best interest.

I'd always told myself that I would find an ordinary man and have an ordinary life.

Somehow I had not noticed that Charlie was an ordinary

man sitting right under my nose. I just hadn't seen him until he brought it to my attention.

So he had asked me to marry him.

I told him I would marry him next spring. I needed time to prepare. I knew it was merely an excuse to put it off, but it satisfied him.

So he came over every day now. It was funny really. I had agreed to marry a man I had never even kissed.

And a day did not pass that I didn't think about Graham. And about his kiss.

I didn't tell anyone, of course. Not Dakota and not Elise. It was one of those things I had to keep to myself. I would take it to my grave.

I was happy I had the memory, though. And I could live off of it.

I would always know that I had experienced a moment of true love. It was more than most people got.

So I did not complain. I had my painting. My family had enough money that we didn't have to worry about anything.

And I had Charlie. My ordinary husband to be.

I dipped my brush in the blue paint on my pallet and added it to the background of my canvas behind the flower. But since it was too close to being the same color blue as the flower, I did some mixing. Played with colors until I got that same color I had created before at Bierstadt Lake. That same lavender blue.

I smiled when I thought about how Dakota had ribbed me about running out of names for my paintings. I suppose I could call this one Lavender Blue Number Two. She would love that. And she would especially love that it proved her point.

Feeling someone watching me, thinking Charlie had showed up or Hector had come outside to bring me a glass of water, I turned, the smile still on my lips.

But it wasn't Charlie and it wasn't Hector.

It was Graham.

I held my brush in midair. Totally forgot what I was doing.

He smiled.

And just like that, my entire world tilted upside down.

Graham had come back.

I slowly set my brush down, while keeping my gaze on his.

I was afraid that if I looked away he would vanish.

Just like Reed had vanished in front of my sister.

Graham was dressed different now and that caught me off guard. He was wearing dark gray pants and a dark gray jacket over a white shirt.

He looked quite handsome really, though his hat was terribly out of style—at least two years—as was his tie.

"What do you think?" he asked, stepping toward me.

"I think I'm going to have to take you shopping," I said.

With both of us taking a step forward, he grabbed me around the waist and, lifting my feet off the ground, twirled me around in a circle.

I was laughing and out of breath by the time he set my feet back on the ground.

He kissed my forehead, then my cheek.

But something surfaced from the back of my mind and I shifted back, biting my bottom lip.

Seeing Graham like this, I had completely forgotten about Charlie.

Charlie.

My betrothed.

CHAPTER 21
GRAHAM

It had taken me ten business days to get my affairs in order. If I was going back to the past, I was going to stay there.

The only door I had left open was my job. My life's dream had been to be a national park ranger. At Rocky Mountain National Park.

So instead of turning in my resignation, I had left a letter. By the time they came looking for me, I would be securely situated in the past.

And, I had decided, being with Bailey trumped being a park ranger. And that was saying everything.

Seeing Bailey sitting there, a princess on a lily pad, had solidified my decision. I'd made the right one.

My heart swelled at seeing her again.

The summer sun was pleasantly warm on my head and the breeze was cooling, making this a perfect summer day.

Wood smoke from the chimney mixed with the clean scent of fir and spruce trees. Chipmunks scurried about looking for food, finding scraps here and there. It seemed that feeding the animals was not just a twenty-first century problem.

What was a problem was the way Bailey pulled back, lowering her eyes.

It was a bit like being kicked in the gut.

I was too late, then.

The ten days it had taken me to prepare everything for moving to the past added on to the time it had taken me to make the decision had been too long.

I squeezed her hand. Or maybe I had misread her interest in me.

But as she looked up at me from beneath her lashes, I saw… indecision and something else.

"You came back," she said, still holding my arms.

"I came back," I said.

"Can you… stay?" she asked.

"Yes. I can stay." It was almost like she knew that I was from another time.

She nodded. "I didn't know. I—" She looked over her shoulder. "Come," she said, tucking a hand in the crook of my elbow and tugging me with her toward the back porch. "We have to talk."

The four words every man dreaded hearing. Those words were never good news.

"Wait," she said. "My painting."

I helped her gather up her canvas and paints. Carefully held the painting by the edges. I'd seen this painting before, I realized.

In the Whiskey Springs library.

"Lavender Blue Number Two," I said.

"What?" She froze, the wind tousling her hair, her eyes bright.

"This painting," I said.

"How could you possibly know that?" she asked, her voice barely audible, with a quick shake of her head.

"Come," I said. "It's part of that talk."

We stepped inside the back door and Dakota nearly dropped the mug she was holding.

She looked from her sister to me and back again.

"He came back," she said.

I was getting the distinct feeling that no one had expected me to come back.

And I had a distinctly sick feeling in the pit of my stomach that something had changed while I was away, taking my time making my decision about what I was going to do.

CHAPTER 22
BAILEY

With the excuse of putting away my paint supplies, I escaped up to my room to give myself a moment to catch my breath.

Facing the window, stood straight. Took a deep breath. Then another.

Mon Dieu.

I had made a mess of things.

A terrible mess.

I had tumbled over in love with Graham the first time I had seen him, but I hadn't trusted the process.

I hadn't given it time to work out.

Instead of waiting. Instead of giving Graham time to come back to me, I had agreed to marry Charlie.

I dropped onto my bed.

Charlie would be over here this afternoon, maybe sooner, and Graham was here.

I didn't know what to do.

I had to tell Graham. I had to tell him before Charlie got here.

There had to be a way to make this right, but I was at a loss.

By the time I got back downstairs, Graham was sitting on the sofa with Colton.

I stood there at the bottom of the stairs, watching them, listening to the steady ticking of the grandfather clock.

Graham looked right. He looked like he fit here.

Charlie always seemed a little uncomfortable around Colton. Or maybe it was just my own uncertainty about Charlie.

"Graham's back," Colton said as I approached the sofa.

"So I heard," I said with a smile at Graham. "He and I need to talk for a minute," I told my brother.

"Just heading out," Colton said. "Catch you later, Graham."

I sat on the sofa next to Graham. Arranged my skirts as I tried to figure out what to tell him.

"Something's wrong," Graham said, looking at me sideways.

"Why would you say that?" I asked before I caught myself. This was not the time to be coy.

I took a deep breath.

"Yes," I said. "Something—"

A knock at the door told me that I had waited too long to tell Graham what was wrong.

Hector opened the door and Charlie came inside. He saw me immediately and smiled. Then he saw Graham sitting next to me and the smile faded from his lips.

Charlie came over and, since there was nowhere else to sit, sat on the chair across from us.

I lifted my chin.

"Charlie," I said. "This is Graham. Graham. Charlie."

The two men shook hands. I sat with my hands clasped in my lap.

"Are you friends with the family?" Charlie asked.

"Yes," Graham said. "I've only just arrived."

"I see," Charlie said. "What brings you here?"

Graham glanced at me.

I smiled at him, then at Charlie.

"I've just made the decision to relocate here," Graham said.

Charlie nodded. "What is it you do?"

"I'm a philanthropist," Graham said. "What do you do?"

"I'm a farmer."

I wanted to separate the two of them. This conversation did not bode well.

But I was at a loss as to how to go about it.

This was nothing like when Drake and Thomas and Charlie had all been here together. They all knew each other and even more importantly, I had not agreed to marry any of them.

But now I had agreed to marry Charlie.

But I wanted to marry Graham.

"Bailey and I are betrothed."

In just the few seconds I had not paid attention to the two men, everything exploded.

CHAPTER 23
GRAHAM

"Congratulations," I said to Charlie, keeping as much emotion out of my voice as I could manage. I knew there was something going on, but I had not anticipated an engagement.

The fire in the fireplace kept the chill out of the house and the scent of muffins in the oven filled the air.

The house was quiet other than the ticking of the grandfather clock and the crackling of the fire. An occasional sound coming from the kitchen as Hector worked.

Things were a bit worse than I expected.

I hadn't considered that Bailey might be engaged to someone else, especially after talking to Vaughn. Vaughn seemed to think that Bailey and I were fated to be together.

I had taken that information and had gone all in.

"You must know the area well," I said to Charlie.

Charlie sat tall in his chair and some of the defensiveness toward me faded, but he continued to watch Bailey. "I know it well enough."

"Do you know of any houses that might be available for sale?"

I felt Bailey tense with a surprised reaction. She, too, was obviously trying to sort through everything.

"There's a place down in Whiskey Springs that's vacant," Charlie said. "On Main Street."

"I kind of like the view up this way," I said.

Charlie shook his head. "I don't know of anything near here."

I would have won the bet on that one. It was natural for Charlie to want me as far away from here as possible.

Elise came down the stairs. Saw me. Grinned.

"Graham." She ran over and took my hands, her full skirt belling out around her. "You came back."

"It's good to see you Elise," I said.

"I knew you would be back." She sat down on the other side of Bailey, inadvertently shoving Bailey closer to me.

Only then did she seem to see Charlie sitting across from us.

"Hello Charlie," she said, still grinning. "Have you met Graham?"

"I have met him," Charlie said.

I forced myself to not share a glance with Bailey.

"He's an old friend of ours," Elise said.

I wasn't sure what to make of Elise. I had spent very little time with her.

But I seemed to remember Bailey telling me that she and Elise were quite close.

At any rate, my admiration for Elise had just increased tenfold.

"He's looking for a house," Bailey said.

"Why?" Elise asked, with a confused frown. "He has a room here."

The clock began to chime the hour.

Everyone sat in silence until the echo of the clock's chimes faded.

"Come," Elise said, jumping up and taking Graham's hand. "Let me show you your room."

Not knowing what else to do, I went with Elise. Followed her up the stairs to what had been my room.

Once we were inside, she left the door open, but looked at me, serious now.

"Bailey didn't think you were coming back."

"So I gathered." I leaned against the door casing, keeping my voice low.

"You were gone a long time," she said.

"I know," I said. "I had some things I had to do."

"But you're not going anywhere this time?" she asked. "Right?"

"Not planning on it," I said. "No matter what Bailey does." I added at her questioning stare.

She nodded slowly. Assessing me.

"Good," she said. "I wouldn't want her to blow up her life if you're not going to be here."

"I'm going to be here."

Elise straightened to her full height. "Are you able to take care of her? Financially?"

I hid a smile behind my hand. "I can take care of her."

"How?" she asked.

"I have family money," I said. Money I wish to God I didn't have. But everyone had insurance and since I was the only heir…

Elise nodded seriously. "I think you should ask Colton for her hand."

I almost laughed, then realized she was serious and remembered what century I was in.

"What about Charlie?"

Elise shrugged. "She isn't married yet."

Then she smiled slowly.

"And she isn't in love with Charlie."

CHAPTER 24
BAILEY

*A*fter Elise dragged Graham away, Charlie moved over to sit next to me.

"Elise seems to like Graham," he said.

"Everyone likes him," I said, fighting down the little tendril of envy that Elise was getting to spend time with Graham while I wasn't.

But I knew that I had made my bed and I had to lie in it, as they said.

"Are you vexed?" Charlie asked.

Sometimes I wished that Charlie didn't pay so much attention to me. He knew me too well.

"A little," I said, looking into the fire.

I was actually very vexed. I had gone and agreed to marry Charlie only because the man I loved had gone back to his own time and I hadn't thought he was coming back.

"What has you vexed?" he asked.

I turned back and looked into Charlie's brown eyes. An ordinary boy. Always here for me. Exactly what I had always said I wanted. But he didn't make my blood race.

Only Graham had that effect on me.

"I'm just tired," I said. "I think I'm going to go up to my room. I need some rest."

"Is there anything I can do to help you feel better?" Charlie asked.

"There's nothing you can do," I said.

He stood up when I did. Leaned over. Kissed me on the cheek.

"Good night Charlie," I said.

I felt awful. I was going to break his heart. But somewhere out there was a girl for him. A girl whose heart would race when she saw him.

Maybe I had been wrong to agree to marry him. Or maybe I had simply been in a self-preservation mode.

Whatever it was, I had to fix it.

With one hand on the railing, holding my swaying skirts with the other, I made my way upstairs.

But if there was one thing I had learned, it was patience. I wasn't going to let go of Charlie until I at least found out what Graham's intentions were.

Sitting on my bed, I looked at the painting of the blue flower I had just finished.

Lavender Blue Number Two.

I smiled. Then on impulse, I turned the painting over and wrote that name on the back of it.

I didn't know how Graham had known that I was thinking about that name.

It was simply something magical. Maybe it was one of those things a girl wasn't supposed to question.

If a man could travel through time, maybe it wasn't such a leap that he would know what I was thinking.

I laid back on the bed and stared at the painting. I'd known I wanted to paint this blue flower, but I hadn't known that it would hold a certain magic for me.

Such a simple little painting. Only about three different

colors blended in, but somehow they worked.

They just worked.

Just like Graham and I worked.

CHAPTER 25
GRAHAM

I almost pleaded fatigue and stayed in my room, but that seemed like the coward's way out.

I'd been through too much to be a coward. There was no room in life for cowardliness. If I'd learned nothing else, I had learned that.

I opened up the wardrobe they had added to the room. It was empty except for my jacket, carefully folded on one of the shelves. My dead cell phone on top of it.

It said something to me that they had kept my things.

I checked my appearance in the mirror. Decided I looked presentable for the time period. I didn't have to wear anyone else's clothes. I did, however, need to make a trip to the tailor sooner than later to have some new clothes made.

I checked the clasp on my wide leather bracelet. Adjusted my matching black leather belt.

Then I headed back into the hallway.

As soon as I stepped outside my door, I saw Bailey coming this way from her end of the hall.

We met at the top of the stairs. We could not have been more in sync if we had planned it.

I grinned at her and blocked her way.

After one unsuccessful attempt to go around me, she stood still and looked at me.

"You said we need to talk," I said.

"I guess there's not much need now," she said, searching my eyes. Her cheeks were flushed prettily.

"I wouldn't mind," I said.

"Okay. I guess we can talk."

"Is there some place up here?" I asked, looking over my shoulder. Not wanting to go downstairs where Charlie waited just yet.

"There's a sitting room," she said.

"Can we use it?"

"Of course," she said.

I followed her back down the hallway and we stepped into what was obviously a lady's sitting area.

There were two chairs in shades of pink in front of a fireplace—no fire. A little basket with needlework. A small writing desk with a stack of paper and an inkwell.

There was a window across from the door and a smaller window on the right wall, but the rest of the walls were covered with paintings. Mountain scenes. Elk. Bierstadt Lake.

I glanced at her then back to the paintings. "Did you do all of these?" I asked.

Following my gaze, she nodded. "All mine."

I walked around the room, stepping closer to better see each one.

"You named them all," I said, over my shoulder.

"Dakota thinks I'm going to run out of names."

I turned and looked at her. "That's where you got *Lavender Blue Number Two.*"

"I was only thinking about that because of what she said." She searched my eyes. "How did you know?"

"Can we sit?" I asked.

We sat next to each other in the chairs. I thought we needed a fire in the fireplace, but I was a guest. I knew how to start a fire without matches, but it didn't seem like my place to bring it up.

"I didn't know what happened to you," she said.

"I need to tell you something," I said. "And it might come as a shock."

"I know you're from the future," she blurted. She sat with her hands clasped in her lap. She didn't look the least bit shocked.

"How do you know that?"

"You remember I have a sister Andrea?"

"Of course. She lives in Denver and is married to Reed Smith." I remembered his photo from the book.

"Well, Reed is from the future."

"What?"

"That's why they can't live here. When he goes through the front door, he goes back to the future. And he has one of those black mirror things. What's that for anyway?"

It took me a minute to absorb everything she was telling me.

The front door was Reed's portal. Bierstadt Lake was mine. He couldn't come here and I could not go back there.

A black mirror?

"It's a phone," I said.

"What's a fawn?" she asked.

"No," I said, trying not to laugh. "The black glass is a device we use for communication. We call it a cell phone." Then I spelled it out for her. "P-H-O-N-E."

"How do you communicate with this phone?"

"I don't even know how to begin to explain it. They somehow carry voices through the air from one to another. So you could use it to talk to your sister in Denver any time you want to."

Her expression brightened. "So since we have one here and she has one, can you make them work?" She stood up. "I'll go get it."

"No," I said, holding up a hand to stop her. "They won't work. There's no tower."

"What kind of tower?" she asked, sitting back down.

"One that hasn't been invented yet."

"Oh." I hated being the cause of that disappointment. I'd do anything to bring the smile back to her face.

"I talked to your sister, Elise."

"What did you talk about?"

"She told me why you agreed to marry Charlie."

"I think Elise talks too much," she said.

"No. I completely understand. I wasn't here. Charlie loves you."

Now I'd put even more sadness on her face.

"I thought I was doing the right thing."

"I know."

"Now I don't know what to do."

"Bailey," I said. "You don't have to do anything right now. I showed up here out of the blue. Without warning. You don't have to upend your life just because I'm here."

She sat back with obvious relief, but the haunted shadows around her eyes remained.

"Thank you," she said.

I leaned forward and took her hands. "I'm sorry I vanished. But I didn't know…"

"It's okay," she said.

"Take your time," I said. "Think it through and decide what you want to do before you do it."

CHAPTER 26
BAILEY

Graham misunderstood me. It wasn't that I didn't know *what* to do. It was that I didn't know *how* to go about it.

After our talk, we went back downstairs.

Elise was sitting on the sofa, reading a book. Dakota sat writing something with one of my charcoal pencils.

I looked around, but didn't see Colton or Charlie.

"Charlie said to tell you he had to go," Elise said with a shrug. "Something about cows."

Charlie's father was giving him more and more responsibility now that he was about to be married.

Another reason for me to feel bad about not marrying Charlie.

"Dinner will be ready in a few minutes," Dakota said.

I sat down next to her, leaving Graham to his own devices. "What are you working on?"

"Nothing," she said, closing her notebook.

"Didn't look like nothing."

"Well, it is."

Graham went into the kitchen.

"What are you going to do about him?" Elise asked.

"What do you mean?"

"You know what she means," Dakota said, holding her notebook close. "Now that you're betrothed to Charlie. And Graham is back."

I stared into the fire, not answering.

"She'll figure it out," Elise said.

"I wish Mama was here," I said. "Or even Andrea."

"I wish that every day," Dakota said. "Doesn't make it happen. You're stuck with us."

She was right, of course. Although I hadn't meant to offend my sisters. I was grateful they were there.

"What would you do?" I asked, looking from one of them to the other."

"I know what I would do," Elise said. "I would tell Charlie that my true love has returned and break it off with him."

She made it sound so easy.

"I would run off with Graham," Dakota said. "Go far away from here."

"You would not," I said. "Besides. I like it here."

"There's nothing to do here," she said.

"Are you kidding?" I asked. "There are more things here than I could ever paint."

"Well," Elise said. "In the meantime, I think you should take Graham shopping. His clothes are terribly outdated."

"They are, aren't they?" I said. For some reason that brought a smile to my lips and lightened my mood.

That was the answer. I'd take him shopping. Tomorrow. Tomorrow we'd go into Whiskey Springs to visit the tailor. I needed to check on my dress anyway. It was supposed to have been ready ages ago.

It would give me a chance to figure things out while spending time with him. Shopping was a good excuse to be with him.

CHAPTER 27
GRAHAM

For some reason Bailey seemed to think that my clothes were outdated. I didn't see it. I'd taken my time doing my research, getting them right.

But apparently 1860s fashion had a lot of variability that I hadn't caught.

We were going to take the buggy down to Whiskey Springs until I had confessed that I didn't know how to drive one.

Bailey admitted that she could drive, but said she didn't want to. She didn't say it, but I got the idea that the man was supposed to drive.

So we walked. It was a pleasant enough walk. About a mile to get there.

The center of the town seemed to be the Whiskey Springs Saloon.

There was also a livery, a general store, and a café.

The tailor, a man named John, and the seamstress had their shops inside the general store.

The tailor, an affable man in his forties, with a terrible haircut, led me behind a curtain to take my measurements.

"How much are you looking to spend?" he asked as he measured my inseam.

"Getting right to the point, I see."

"No point in wasting time," John said. "I already have more business than I can handle."

"I don't think money is going to be an object," I said.

John moved to measure my arms. "Not a very specific answer," he said.

"How specific do I need to be?" I put my arms down and put my jacket back on.

John began winding up his tape measure. "Miss Bailey said you'll be needing quite a few items as soon as possible."

"That's right," I said. "My trunks were destroyed during a river crossing." I had rehearsed that one.

"Hmph."

Apparently that wasn't good enough for John.

"Do you have a small knife?" I asked.

John reached behind him. Picked up a knife off the counter. Handed it to me.

"Thank you," I said.

Turning my back to him, I unclasped my leather bracelet and, stretching it out on a table, turned it over. Carefully using the knife, I traced the point along the first little rectangular seam.

If this didn't work, I didn't know what I was going to do. It had to work.

A minute later, I put my bracelet back on and returned the knife.

"How much will this get me?" I held up the little piece of gold I had just taken from my bracelet.

John lifted his glasses from a string around his neck. Peered at the gold piece.

"Mr. Daniels," he said, dropping his glasses. "You tell me

what you would like to have and I will have everything completed for you posthaste. Starting tomorrow."

I grinned. Apparently gold was as valuable here as history indicated.

And I had no shortage.

That was just one small piece. My belt was lined with larger, heavier pieces of gold. Had some silver, too, just for good measure.

"Make sure all my pants have belt loops," I said.

"Of course, Sir," he said. "What should I do with the balance?"

"Can you share it with the seamstress?"

"That can be arranged."

"Then use it for anything she owes and anything she want to order. We'll figure out what to do with the rest."

A man with means could have a much easier life than a man without means. That was a universal fact no matter which century a man lived in.

Looks like converting all my insurance money into gold and silver had been the right move.

Now all I had to do was to convince Bailey that I was the better choice for a husband.

CHAPTER 28
BAILEY

After picking out several outfits for John to make for Graham, we picked up my dress from the seamstress.

"Put it on my balance and I'll settle up later," I said.

The seamstress, a young lady of French descent by the name of Marie smiled. "Your account has been settled," she said. "And when you're ready, we can pick out some other patterns and cloth."

"Okay," I said. Maybe Colton had taken care of everything. He'd been working on the accounts lately.

Marie smiled at Graham. "She's beautiful, yes?"

"Without question."

"And a joy to make beautiful dresses for her."

"Anything she wants," he said.

Graham picked up the box with my dress and we left the general store.

"What was that about?" I asked.

Graham just shrugged and changed the subject. "Let's get some lunch," he said.

We went into the café and he held my chair while I sat.

"Thank you," I said, then leaned close. "Is this something men do in the future? Holding a lady's chair?"

"Rarely," he said. "But I did some reading. I'm sure there are things I won't know about. You'll help me though, right?"

"Of course," I said, enjoying the thought of helping Graham navigate things that were in his past. Things he wouldn't be familiar with.

"Surely it's not all that different," I said, thinking about the history that I had studied.

Graham looked away for a moment, then back. "It's so strange. From about the middle of the twentieth century to when I lived in the early twenty-first century, the world seemed to completely change."

"How so?"

"Cell phones. Horseless carriages. Airplanes."

I just looked blankly at him. He might as well be talking a different language.

"It's too much to even begin to describe. It's much more peaceful here. Now."

The server brought our water.

"I'll have your food right out," the server said.

"I don't remember ordering," he said.

"They just bring out whatever they have."

"No choices?"

"Sometimes. But apparently not today. Do you get choices?"

"Some places have menus that are like books," he said. "There's this place called the Cheesecake Factory."

"Well," I said. "I didn't realize there were that many things to eat."

"People got creative."

The server brought out our plates. We were having mashed potatoes, biscuits, and slabs of ham.

"Do you think Hector would let me use the kitchen some?" Graham asked.

"Or course," I said, taking a bite of mashed potatoes. "It's our house."

"I have an idea. Something I can cook that you just might like."

"What is it?"

"Pizza."

I grinned. "This is going to be fun."

CHAPTER 29
GRAHAM

*A*fter lunch, we started home.

Piano music spilled out of the saloon, but, nonetheless, the little town seemed tame enough.

Women and children walked from place to place on the streets.

The sounds of construction were everywhere. Mostly hammering.

Lunch was a bit disappointing, but it had given me the idea of making pizza. I was pretty sure I could do it.

I was thinking through what we might need.

"I need to make a quick stop by the General Store," I said. Maybe they had tomato sauce in a jar. My research into the past hadn't gone in this direction.

We stepped inside. The General Store had everything. Scented candles. Jars of hard candy. Bolts of material.

Cans of whitewash for painting. Newspapers. Jewelry.

"What are we looking for?" she asked.

"It's a surprise," I said.

She looked up at me with such an irresistible, impish grin

that I could not resist. I leaned over and kissed her on the cheek.

"Bailey?"

We both turned and came face to face with Charlie.

He looked at both us. Both grinning.

"What is this?"

"Nothing," Bailey said. "I was just—"

"I saw you kiss her," Charlie said, his voice full of disbelief.

My stomach dropped. It was a simple kiss on the cheek. Something innocent enough. Even for one's mother or sister.

But this was a different time and a kiss on the cheek meant something else entirely.

"Please accept my apologies," I said, taking a step back. "I was out of bounds." The last thing I needed was trouble.

"Bailey is my betrothed," Charlie said. "It's my job to protect her honor."

"Charlie," Bailey said, putting a hand on Charlie's arm. "My honor was never in danger."

"I saw what I saw," Charlie said, his chin jutting out. "I demand satisfaction."

"Satis—" Good God. The man was challenging me to a duel.

"No," I said, taking another step back. "I won't do it."

"You're a coward," Charlie said.

I shook my head. There was no way for me to win this one. I could not fight him and be branded a coward or I could fight and one of us would die.

"Look," I said. "Let's find a more civilized way to resolve this."

"A duel is civilized," he said then added with a spat. "Sir."

"Alright. Fine," I said.

"No," Bailey said. "He's right. There's got to be a more civilized way to resolve this."

"You take his side," Charlie said. "I should have known. I did know. In my gut I knew. You were never going to marry me.

"Charlie."

Charlie turned on his heel and stomped out of the store.

Bailey looked at me, her chest heaving, her eyes bright. She was angry, I realized.

"Fix it," she said, twirling around, her skirts brushing against me, and left the store.

I stood there at the door and watched them. Charlie stomped off in one direction and Bailey headed the other way toward home.

Fix it.

How the hell was I supposed to fix this?

Well, hell.

The first thing I had to do was to make sure she got home safely.

CHAPTER 30
BAILEY

*I*t was going to rain.

Go figure.

One of the best days had circled around to be one of the worst days.

The rain started before I was even a third of the way home. It was just a light summer afternoon shower, but it soaked me through and through anyway.

I brushed at the angry tears at first, then gave up since my tears blended with the rain.

I wasn't even sure what I was angry about.

Myself, mostly.

I had done this to myself.

I wasn't in love with Charlie, but I didn't want him to get hurt.

I was in love with Graham though. Didn't Charlie understand that if he killed Graham, I would never want to see his face again?

Charlie could not win this one. He would either be dead or he would be banned from my life.

He was a stupid, stupid man.

I should never ever have agreed to marry him.

Now someone was going to be killed.

Stupid men.

Why did they have to be so stupid?

I needed to think. I needed to figure this out.

Charlie was being irrational and Graham didn't understand. I couldn't expect him to understand.

I went in through the front door of the house, slammed the door for no reason. There was no one here.

I went up to my room. Dried off and changed into my light green dress.

Taking my sketch pad, I went to the sitting room at the end of the hall.

If I didn't have to share it with my sisters, it would be a great studio for my painting.

It wouldn't be right though, to take a whole room for myself.

I paced from one side of the room to the other. My boots clicked on the wood, then went silent as I walked over the wool rug in the middle of the floor. Then back on the floor.

Stopped at the window and looked down.

The rain had naturally stopped. Stopping just as quickly as it had started and lasting just long enough to make a mess of everything.

A blue bird sat on a tree limb outside my window and looked at me.

"What do I do?" I asked the bird.

The bird just flew off.

Well that just figured.

The problem was there was no way to fix this.

I should have just told Charlie up front about Graham.

That would have kept this from happening to begin with.

I fell into one of the pink chairs and stared at the fireplace.

With a huff, I knelt in front of the hearth and built a fire.

There. Much better.

Nothing was more depressing than a fireplace with no fire.

I sat back in my chair and picked up my sketchpad. Turned to a fresh page.

I began sketching nothing in particular. Just marks on the page.

Letting my thoughts go blank.

As I wielded the charcoal pencil, I calmed down.

Sketching did that to me. It was the one thing that could set me right when I was off-balance.

I was definitely off-balance right now.

I stopped and tapped my finger against the canvas.

There had to be a way to stop the men from killing each other.

All I had to do was to figure it out.

CHAPTER 31
GRAHAM

I heard the door slam twenty yards away.

All Bailey had to do was to turn around and she would see that I was right behind her.

But she was too upset to bother.

I went in through the front door and straight to the kitchen. No one was home.

The house was quiet except for the steady ticking of the grandfather clock.

By the time I got back in the parlor, I could hear Bailey pacing back and forth in one of the rooms upstairs. The lady's sitting room, perhaps.

I needed Colton.

I didn't know much about dueling. What I did know, I'd gotten from the movies.

I was pretty sure I needed a second. Someone to watch out for my interests.

Another thing. I was pretty sure dueling was illegal.

Going to jail was not what I had come back through time for.

Bailey and I had had such a good day together.

That was what I had come here for. To be with her.

And she was everything and more than I had anticipated. She was delightful.

I needed to put on dry clothes, but I didn't have anything else to wear. If I had been smart, I would have brought extra clothes.

Going upstairs to my room, I dried off as best I could. Fortunately, my hat had protected me from getting completely soaked. Wondered how long it would be before Bailey kicked me out of here.

I had no reason to think she would choose me over Charlie.

Charlie was more her age. A younger fellow. Knew his way around Whiskey Springs. Probably had a good-sized farm where he could take Bailey to live. They could raise a few kids and be happy.

Then here I come, making a mess of all that.

She wouldn't have any reason to trust me.

As far as she knew, I was a fly by night kind of guy. Here today. Gone tomorrow. It certainly felt like that to me and I wasn't her.

I went back downstairs to look for Colton.

The hell of it was that she already knew I was from the future and it didn't bother her one bit.

Vaughn was right. Bailey and I were perfect for each other.

But how was I going to get myself out of this pickle?

If I killed Charlie, Bailey would never talk to me again. If Charlie killed me—a more likely scenario—then... what was the point of me even being here?

She'd tried to talk Charlie out of it.

But then she'd turned on me.

Told me to fix it.

I wasn't sure what to make of that.

The first thing I had to do was to find Colton. Colton will know the rules of this whole dueling thing.

I hadn't brought my gun with me. Hadn't seen much point in it when I could buy a new one. One that I could actually buy bullets for.

I went outside. Sat on the front steps to wait for Colton.

An hour later, Colton rides in from town. He slid off his horse and tied it to the hitching post.

Walked over and, putting his hands on his waist, looks at me.

"You've got something of a problem," he said.

"So it seems." And it did not surprise me that the whole town knew about this duel challenge.

"You need my help."

"I do need your help."

Colton walked over and sat on the steps next to me. "Before I help you, I need to know something."

"I'll tell you what I know."

"Two things," Colton said.

"Go ahead," I said.

Colton took off his hat. "Are you from the future."

"Yes," I said.

"John tells me you have gold."

"Brought it with me."

"Then you're set."

"As long as gold has value," I said. I'd only given John one small piece of gold. John was acting like I gave him a set of gold bars.

"You want to marry my sister."

I couldn't tell if that was a question or a comment.

"Elise said I should ask you for her hand," I said.

"Nobody's asked me," he said.

"Charlie?"

"Like I said. Nobody has asked me."

"Well, that's convenient."

"Could be."

"Colton," I said. "I'd like to marry your sister. Bailey. Do I have your permission?"

Colton didn't answer right away. I didn't really have a back-up plan if he said no.

"We have to get you out of this mess," he said. "Then, yes, you have my permission to marry Bailey."

"Thank you."

"But there's one thing."

"Sure." Wasn't there always something?

"You have to do what you have to do to stay in this time. Can't be disappearing on her."

"That's my intent."

"I mean it. If you do, I'll… I'll post it in every newspaper that you're a scoundrel. I'll make sure it shows up in every history book."

I smiled to myself at Colton's creativity. It must run in his family. "Understood."

"Good," he said.

"Good."

Colton stood up. "Come to my study after dinner. We'll work out the details for tomorrow's duel."

"I'll be there."

Colton went inside, leaving me sitting there on the steps.

With nothing better to do, I took his horse around and put him in the stable.

No matter what Colton said, there was no way I was going to kill Charlie.

The thing was I could do it. I could kill him.

I was a damn good shot.

CHAPTER 32
BAILEY

$\mathcal{U}$p before dawn, I dressed by candlelight. As always, it was chilly. Even in summer.

But I'd take the cold over the muggy Mississippi summers that never cooled down to a comfortable level even in the middle of the night.

My fingers trembled as I slipped into a pale silver riding habit. I had more riding habits than regular gowns these days. I liked their versatility for not only riding, but walking and sitting on the ground when I wanted to paint or sketch.

I sat on my vanity bench and tugged on my boots. Laced them up tightly.

I had hardly slept at all last night. I had tossed and turned. Fretted.

Dakota and Elise and I had supper sent up and ate in our lady's parlor. We'd had lunch up there a few times, but never supper. It felt… disruptive to the family.

I did not want to face Graham right now simply because I didn't know what to say to him.

But I had my spies. Dakota had found out and reported

everything I needed to know about this morning's duel. Well, everything except the exact location.

Nonetheless, it seemed as though they were actually going through with it.

Insanity.

I brushed my hair, then pulled it back and secured it at the back of my head.

I studied my appearance in the mirror as best I could in the candlelight.

Stupid men.

I put on my fur-lined cloak, pulled the hood over my head, then slipped out into the dark hallway. I went downstairs and quietly made my way out the back door.

The biting wind made it even colder outside.

I hurried into the stable. Tossed a saddle over my mare, a gentle creature named Grace.

The word was that Graham and Charlie were going to ride to a field somewhere on the other side of Whiskey Springs and have their duel at dawn. Duels were always at dawn. Supposedly to give the men time to come to their senses. Right now I wasn't sure men had any sense at all.

With Grace saddled and ready, I hid in the stall behind her and waited.

It was only a few minutes later when Graham and Colton came in and quietly saddled their own horses.

Then they were off and I was right behind them, only the meager first break of dawn lighting our way.

I had to stay back, lest they see me. Fortunately I had a good idea where they were headed. Besides, they would never expect anyone to follow.

I still didn't know what I was going to do. I only knew that I could not allow the two men to shoot at each other.

One of them was my friend. The other one was the one I wanted to marry.

But somehow that had gotten reversed. Charlie thought I would marry him. I wasn't sure what Graham thought.

We reached town, rode down Main Street, past the closed saloon. I had never seen the saloon with its doors shuttered and no sounds spilling out.

It was eerie.

I wanted this be over. To go home. For everyone to live in peace.

I would do whatever it would take to make that happen.

Whatever it takes.

After following the two men through town, they turned down what looked like no more than a path. This was where I had to keep up in order to not lose them.

I nudged Grace into a trot in order to catch up. Just as we turned off the main road, with a little cry, Grace's front right hoof slid. She managed to catch herself, keeping herself on her feet and keeping me from falling off.

I had to stop. Grace was limping.

I slid off her back and picked up her hoof. It was too dark to see. But she pulled back when I lightly touched the bottom of her foot.

There was no way I could ride her now. She was in pain.

I guided Grace away from the trail. Found a tree with a low hanging limb and tied her up.

"I'm sorry, Grace," I said, patting her neck. "I'll be back as soon as I can. I have to go stop a couple of idiot men from killing each other."

I could take her with me, but that would make her have to walk unnecessary steps. It was going to be bad enough for her to have to walk all the way back to the blacksmith.

Gathering up my skirts, I continued down the path. The terrain was uneven now. Rocky.

I had to slow down to keep from throwing a shoe myself.

Fortunately, the sun was growing higher with every minute.

I had to slow down even more as I crossed a little rivulet with early morning mist hovering over it.

Mon Dieu. I hope I was going the right way. For all I knew I was lost.

Even if was going the right way, the duel would be over before I got there.

And the two stupid men would have already killed each other.

CHAPTER 33
GRAHAM

The dew sparkled in the early morning sunlight.

Any other day, in any other situation, it would have looked magical.

Surrounded by majestic and rugged mountain peaks, this was a valley. A valley I didn't remember seeing before.

Probably private property now… in the future…

When Colton and I arrived at the designated dueling spot, Charlie was already there standing with an older man.

"That's his father," Colton told me as we neared the two men.

Another fellow stood not far from them.

"Who's that?"

"That's Doc Avery."

I'd heard that name. Doc Avery was one of the founders of Whiskey Springs.

"This must be serious," I mused for the doctor to be there.

"A duel is always a serious matter," Colton said. Colton seemed older than his years. He was the middle child. Two older sisters and two younger sisters.

He was younger than Bailey, but not by more than a year.

The Auclair siblings were spaced in enviable precision. Almost like their parents had planned them.

But was that even possible in the 1800s? Possible, sure, but not likely.

Doc Avery stood off by himself. According to Colton, the Doc did not condone dueling, but he also did not condone letting men die unnecessarily.

We slid off our horses and tied them off.

"Are you sure I can't just apologize?"

"Charlie isn't accepting that," Colton said. "Just do what we said."

"Have you talked to his father yet?"

"I'll talk to him now," Colton said. "You wait here."

I watched as Colton marched right over to Charlie and his father. They left Charlie standing there and walked away from everyone else.

I couldn't hear a word they were saying. I just hoped that Charlie's father was less hot-headed than Charlie and had more sense about him than his son did.

The sun was bright and with each minute, it got a little bit brighter.

I wanted this mess to just be over.

If Bailey wanted to marry Charlie, then so be it.

It just meant it wasn't our time yet.

It did not mean that I would be giving up on her though.

I had survived that plane crash on my wedding day for a reason.

And I had traveled to the past for a reason.

I had to believe that it all meant something.

Surely it wasn't all for naught.

Colton and Charlie's father walked back to where they had left the weapons.

I crossed my arms and waited. I was at the mercy of these men.

If they decided that Charlie and I should shoot at each other, then that's what we would do. Even though I knew it was stupid, I did not want to go through this world branded as a coward without honor. I was not a coward. And I would not have Bailey believing that I was.

Colton turned and nodded in my direction, indicating that I should join him.

"Sir," I said to Charlie's father.

The man merely nodded at me, not saying anything.

"Choose one of the weapons," Colton said.

"There's no way to stop this?" I asked. "No acceptable apology?"

"Just choose a weapon," Colton said. "And trust in the process."

Trust in the process. Whatever the hell that meant.

I picked up one of the guns.

It was heavy in my hand.

And for the first time since this fiasco started, I felt a shiver of genuine fear. I was a good shot. But the guns I was familiar with were significantly lighter and easier to handle.

This pistol was far heavier than anything I was used to.

Doc Avery walked over.

"I'll take it from here," he told us. He then instructed for Charlie and me to stand back to back.

This felt surreal, like being in a movie.

"On my mark, take ten paces. Stop. And await my instructions."

I held the gun in my hands. Wondered if I had come to the past only to die.

Maybe I was already dead.

Maybe I had lost touch with reality.

That, I decided was most likely.

How else would I end up in a field at dawn? About to be

fired upon because I kissed a girl on the cheek? And not just any girl. The girl I had come to the past to live my live with.

But that girl was engaged—betrothed—to the man about to shoot me.

I had no doubt that Charlie was going to shoot me. He had come this far and he wouldn't want to look like a coward either.

As long as we did not get caught, a duel was perfectly legal. And apparently this was the spot where men came to shoot at each other.

"Take ten paces," Doc Avery said. "Now."

I began walking as instructed. Ten paces.

That put twenty steps between us. Not far enough as far as I was concerned. It would be hard to miss.

But considering that I had never fired one of these guns, all bets were off.

I had to remind myself that no matter what, I was not going to pull the trigger. I was not going to take a man's life over such a trivial matter. And truly Charlie was too young to understand the implications.

He had not lost everyone like I had.

"Turn and fire," Doc Avery said.

"Stop!" As I turned, I caught a glimpse of Bailey, running toward us, silver skirts flying behind her.

My attention was on her now. Not on Charlie.

Out of the corner of my eye, I saw him lift his weapon.

But before I had time to process what was happening, Bailey was standing in front of me.

"No," she said, fiercely. "If you want to shoot someone, Charlie, shoot me."

Charlie slowly lowered his weapon.

My gun was still at my side.

It began to sink in that Bailey was protecting me, not Charlie.

"The duel is hereby forfeited," Doc Avery said. "Due to danger of a lady."

I didn't know if that was a real thing or not, but no one questioned Doc Avery.

Colton took the gun from my hand while his father took Charlie's.

Looked like we had both survived the duel.

"Let's go home," Colton said.

CHAPTER 34
BAILEY

My heart pounded in my chest so hard I could barely catch my breath.

I watched as Charlie and his father mounted their horses and rode off.

I grieved a little bit at the loss of my friendship with Charlie. He and I had spent a lot of time together over the past few weeks.

But that friendship was over.

Charlie had tolerated Thomas and Drake, but he found Graham to be a threat. I understood it.

Besides the fact that I had agreed to marry Charlie, an idiot could no doubt see that I had feelings for Graham.

Every idiot except for Graham himself.

"That's it?" Graham asked. "It's over?"

"A bit anticlimactic, isn't it?" Colton asked.

"Just be glad it's over," I said.

"How did you get here?" Colton asked, looking pointedly at me.

"I rode Grace," I said. "But she threw a shoe, so I had to leave her behind."

"We need to go get her," he said. "Before a bear does."

All three of us walked to their horses.

"Can I hitch a ride?" I asked.

"Graham?" Colton asked.

"Sure," Graham said.

He wasn't saying much. But there was time for talking later.

Graham climbed onto his horse, then pulled me up into his lap.

Being this close to him was a bit unexpected and had my thoughts scattered.

We rode in silence side by side with Colton. Graham had his arm around me and I was pressed against his chest.

"I'm going to ride ahead," Colton said. "Check on Grace."

Without waiting for a reply, he nudged his horse ahead, leaving me with Graham.

I held my hands together tightly, wrapped around the saddle horn, feeling a bit nervous.

"Are you okay?" Graham asked.

"I think so," I said. "Are you?" I looked back at him over my shoulder.

"I'm better now," he said. "I won't lie about that."

"Why would you lie?" I asked, with a little laugh. "You don't have to lie to me."

A marmot sat the side of the trail, watching us. Pigeons darted over, looking for something to eat. Sometimes I fed them bread crumbs, but not today.

The day was most definitely looking better than it had started.

"I know we talked before, but it seems like maybe things have changed since then," he said.

"I guess they have changed," I said. "I only agreed to marry Charlie because I didn't think... didn't know... if you were coming back."

"You knew I was from the future," he said.

"Not for certain until you told me. But, yes. I knew."

We crossed the little rivulet. The mist had cleared and it was much easier to navigate on the back of a horse.

"I think you knew before I did," he said.

"You must have been very confused."

I couldn't imagine what it would be like to find myself in another time. And it wasn't something I wanted to find out.

"I was confused," he said. "I've had a lot of things happen to me in the last year or so. Things that have changed my life."

"Good things?"

"You're the only bright spot." He straightened in the saddle. "Even getting the job I had always wanted wouldn't have been enough."

"You gave it up."

"Happily," he said. "I didn't even know you were what I wanted until I found you."

I smiled to myself. I felt the same way.

"What now?" I asked.

"Good question," he said. "I guess I have some business to take care of before I can do much else."

I nodded. Business wasn't really what I wanted to talk about.

"You understand about Charlie? Right?"

"You mean being engaged to him? Of course I do. You had to take care of yourself."

"It's just… He was a good friend, you know."

"Bailey," he said. "You don't have to justify anything to me. but there is something you need to know."

He tightened his hold on me and kissed the top of my head. "I guess I can do this now without getting myself killed."

"Yes," I said on a little laugh. "I certainly hope so. What is it you want me to know?"

"You won't have to worry anymore. You won't have to ever marry someone you don't want to."

"What do you mean?"

"Let me take care of my business," he said. "Then we'll talk again."

Men had to take care of their business.

If Graham was any indication, that hadn't changed over time.

I relaxed again him.

At least the duel was over and no one had been hurt.

CHAPTER 35
GRAHAM

I took Colton with me to Boulder City—the early city of Boulder. Maybe I should say he took me. Surprisingly enough, he not only knew where to go, he even knew people here.

Boulder was a bustling town with lots of saloons. Lots of shopping. Lots of places to eat. The people here seemed to be busy as bees.

There were lots of banks, too, and we spent a lot of time there. Sitting at desk. Talking to wealthy, powerful men. There was less paperwork than in the future, but getting gold appraised took a lot of time.

Then I had some things to buy. A good horse. A buggy.

And land.

Buying land required me to ride back up into the mountains after studying a map. Things looked a whole lot different on their maps than on the maps I was familiar with.

I figured I could have helped them out on those maps, but as an independently wealthy man, I wasn't committing to anything just yet. It was good to have something to fall back on.

But I had a wife to procure and a house to build.

Sitting on the top of a mountain looking down over the little town of Whiskey Springs, I decided that this was the place. It had unparalleled views.

I could see the side of Long's Peak from here. A good view of the valley below with the river. And on a clear day, we'd be able to see all the way to Denver.

And what with having an artist for a wife that was of utmost importance. Views. Wildlife. Lots of space inside and out.

I was going to build a castle. Why not? According to the bankers I had met with, I had more money than any one man could ever spend in a lifetime. A wealthy, powerful man in my own right.

I was happy to pick that up as a challenge.

Maybe I would buy some good horses. Breed them. My grandfather had done that once upon a time, so it would be in his honor. Besides, I found it interesting.

I had lots of options.

And lots of things I had to do. I had to hire an architect. My sister had been in college, studying to be an architect, before the accident, so that one caused a hitch in my mood. I had to tamp that one down deep and keep going.

I'd bring in a plumber. I'd been told I would have to send for someone back east. That was okay. We were going to have indoor plumbing, whatever it took.

And I had to buy a diamond ring.

Then propose to the girl of my dreams.

That was the most important part.

Even if I hadn't had insurance money that had ironically exploded in value by bringing it to the past, that would still have been foremost on my mind. I would have found a way to make a life for us.

All I wanted was for the two of us to be happy.

To wake up with Bailey every morning. To spend my days with her.

We'd grow old together.

And I'd most certainly keep myself away from Bierstadt Lake.

I was like Reed, Andrea's husband, in that way.

He had taken his wife and moved to Denver.

I was taking my wife and building a house on top of a mountain.

Like was good.

CHAPTER 36
BAILEY

By the time Graham was gone for four days, I was fit to be tied.

Fortunately, Colton was with him, so I didn't have to worry too much about his safety. Colton knew how to navigate his way in Boulder City.

If Graham and I had been married, I could have gone with them and probably could have anyway since Colton was there, but I didn't.

My little garden was in full bloom and since I didn't have Charlie helping me anymore, it all fell on me.

Not that I minded. I liked the scent of the earth. The scent of new plants. I liked watching them grow.

And every day I found something new to paint on a canvas.

I had plenty of time—maybe too much—to imagine how my days would be different once I was married to Graham.

Of course, I thought as I pulled weeds from around my carrot plants, he had not asked me yet.

But if the way he looked at me was any indication, I was fairly certain that it would happen.

He'd kissed me again, too. On the lips. I played that simple kiss over and over a million times in my head.

Such a little thing, probably, but I couldn't stop thinking about it. Imagining what it would like to be in his arms. To spend every day with him.

I imagined it would be wonderful.

I stood up, straightened, and looked down toward the river. An elk had wandered over to the bank and raised his head as I did. He twitched his ears, then bent his head and went back to drinking.

I took off my hat and turned my face up to the sun. It was so pleasantly warm, but I knew how quickly my skin could burn.

The scent of the spruce and fir trees was strong today. Always was after the afternoon rain showers. It was like rain washed off the dust, making them fresh.

I looked down the road like I did a thousand times a day.

I watched for Graham and Colton. I couldn't help it and I didn't fight it. Elise and Dakota could make fun of me all they wanted.

Blinking, I stood perfectly still. Colton was riding around the bend.

I waited. Counted to ten. And watched. Graham should be right behind him.

But as Colton neared the house, I knew he was alone.

Gathering up my skirts, I walked quickly to head him off before he reached the stable.

"Where is Graham?" I asked. I could barely speak, I was so overcome with worry.

"Good to see you, too, Sis," he said, sliding off his horse.

"Where is he?" I looked down the road again.

"He'll be along in a few days," Colton said as though it was no big deal whatsoever.

"Why? Is he... okay?" Had he gone through time again?

"He's good. He had to go into Denver to meet with someone."

"Why didn't you go with him?" I asked.

"Things to do here," he said, taking his horse's reins and leading him inside.

I followed.

"Well," I asked. "What is he doing?"

Colton looked me. I swear a little smile crossed his features before he caught it.

"He doesn't tell me everything," Colton said.

I crossed my arms in frustration. "When is he coming back?"

"Give him a couple of days," Colton said with a little laugh. "He'll be here."

Colton just did not understand. He didn't understand about time travel. Anything could happen to Graham.

"He's okay," Colton said.

"Right," I agreed, taking a breath. "He'll be okay."

I wanted to believe Colton. Had no choice really.

Graham had promised he would be back.

He had even promised that I would be taken care of.

I told myself he wouldn't make those kinds of promises if he didn't mean it.

Giving up on getting any more information from my brother, I went inside to clean up.

Maybe I'd do some sketching. That usually helped me when I was feeling antsy like this.

Men.

They were going to be the death of me yet.

CHAPTER 37
BAILEY

Two night later I sat alone in my room. Thunder crashed outside, shaking the very foundation of the house.

I sat at my little writing desk in front of the window, working by the light of two candles.

My little leather journal lay open in front of me.

I dipped my quill into the little ink pot and carefully wrote the date.

July 23, 1867

My journal was my secret. I had started writing in it when I was a youngster. I only wrote down things on occasion. When something struck me as significant in my life.

I wanted to remember. And if I ever had children, I would let them read my journal. Maybe. Maybe not.

It held my innermost thoughts. Things I kept to myself and didn't even share with my sisters. Especially didn't share with my sisters.

Sometimes I wrote down things to help me understand them.

Like now.

I was so worried about Graham. Worried that he had gone back to the future and I would never see him again.

This wasn't about Charlie. Charlie had been a mistake I wouldn't make again.

I would never again agree to marry someone just because it seemed like the right thing to do.

I would only agree to marry someone I was in love with.

The thing was I couldn't see me ever being in love with anyone other than Graham.

A bolt of lightning crashed into the room, lighting everything up for a brief second.

Elise was afraid when there was a thunderstorm, but I found the storms beautiful.

I wasn't afraid of them. I wasn't afraid of much.

Except never seeing Graham again. I was most definitely afraid of that.

I wrote that in my journal.

I have a fear. A fear that I won't ever see Graham again.

Sitting back, I studied my own words.

It seemed crazy. I barely even knew Graham. And he was from the future, for God's sake. I couldn't do anything the easy way.

I sighed, thinking about my sister Andrea. She sent regular letters and she seemed so happy. She and Reed were expecting a baby soon.

Maybe Graham and I would go visit them.

There. That.

How had he gotten so deep into my thoughts?

Because we were meant to be.

I don't know where the thought came from, but it seemed so foreign, that I looked over my shoulder to make sure I was still alone.

I shivered and pulled my shawl closer around my shoulders.

So now I was hearing voices.

Maybe I am crazy.

I smiled to myself. Maybe I was. But it was a good kind of crazy.

There was a commotion downstairs. I put away my ink and waited for the words to dry on the page before I closed my journal.

I should go downstairs. See what was happening. Isolation was a precursor to being crazy. Maybe I just needed to head it off.

When I stepped out into the hallway, I noticed that it was unusually quiet. My siblings were not quiet by nature. They talked. They laughed.

But now they were quiet. Maybe they had all gone outside.

The only sound other than the thunder was the steady ticking of the grandfather clock.

We had brought the clock with us from Mississippi. It was the only thing other than our trunks that had survived the trip west. There had been times when I didn't think the clock was going to make it either.

But it did. It had a scar across its face, a rip between the six and seven, but was otherwise intact. The old clock seemed like part of the family.

I'd never known life without it.

I reached the top of the stairs and noticed that downstairs was lit by candlelight. If they had all gone outside, they surely would not have left the candles burning. Not unless it was an emergency.

Could be the horses, I thought.

Hurrying now, in case I could be of assistance, I gathered up my skirts and walked down the stairs.

Halfway down I saw him.

Graham was standing there, in the middle of the room. He grinned at me.

I looked around, but didn't see anyone else.

"They're in the kitchen," he said.

"Oh." I put a hand to my chest, forcing my heart rate to slow to a normal rate. One that wouldn't cause my heart to explode.

"You're back," I said.

"Did you miss me?" he asked.

"Maybe."

He met me at the bottom of the stairs.

Grabbed me at the waist and twirled me around.

Then he set me on my feet.

"Well, I missed you," he said. "I didn't even get everything done, so I'll have to go back."

"Oh." My heart dropped.

"You can come with me."

"I can't—" He put a finger lightly on my lips.

"You can do anything you want to do."

My eyes wide, I just looked at him. He was acting funny.

"But first…"

He dropped to the floor and took both my hands in his, kissed the backs of my fingers. My palm.

"Bailey," he said. He took a diamond ring out of his pocket and held it up.

"Will you marry me?"

A flash of lightning lit up the room, followed by a deafening clap of thunder.

I couldn't answer. I wanted to. But I couldn't get my words out. So I just nodded.

He slipped the ring on my finger.

"Do you like it?" he asked. It was a beautiful solitaire diamond on a plain silver band. Very simple.

"I love it," I said on a breath.

"Does that mean yes?"

I looked into his eyes. His beautiful sky-blue eyes.

"Yes," I said, wrapping my arms around him.

A proposal born in a storm had to mean forever.

EPILOGUE

With a gloved hand tucked in Graham's elbow, I walked through the halls of what could only be called a castle in the mountains.

The house had eight bedrooms, each bedroom having what Graham called an *en suite*. Each one of the bedrooms had its own bathtub and its own toilet. He had paid an engineer to come all the way from Boston to design the system.

No one out here had ever seen anything like this.

"What are we going to do with eight bedrooms?" I asked as Graham and I walked hand in hand upstairs to the third floor.

"Since the large one is on the second floor, that will be ours, of course. The other two will be guest rooms."

"That leaves five bedrooms," she said, looking over at me sideways.

I grinned. "You know what the other five are for. There are five of you. Why shouldn't we have five?"

She blushed prettily. "Ambitious, are we?"

"Wait until you see what I have for you on the fourth floor. It's the only floor I furnished and that was to surprise you. But we can change it however you want."

We went there next. The fourth floor was open with glass views on all four sides and a wide wrap-around balcony already furnished with chairs and tables. It had a huge fireplace in the center that opened on two sides.

I twirled around, looking at the room in amazement. It was already filled with cubbies for paints and canvases.

Then I went to one of the windows and took in the view. It was magnificent. It had views of rugged mountain peaks. Valleys. Meadows. It truly felt like it was on top of the world. And there, spread out in the valley below was Whiskey Springs.

"It's your studio," he said.

Sprinting back to him, grinning ear to ear, I stood right in front of him, taking hold of his collar in both hands. "You're just putting me up here out of your way."

"Now why would I do that when we have so many rooms to fill? Besides..." he pointed to an open workroom with a desk behind me.

"That is where I'll be working while you paint. So you may as well get used to me watching you."

"Maybe I like it when you watch," I said.

"Then I'd say we are the perfect couple and may have to build even more bedrooms onto the house."

I swiped at him and turned around, taking it all in.

But... I bit my lip. There was one thing that troubled me. With all the windows, there was very little wall space. Just two rooms on one side, one of them an en suite.

"What's troubling you, love?"

"Where will I put my finished paintings?" I mused.

"Every room on the first three floors of the house will be covered with your paintings. In fact, that will be your challenge. Paper the walls, my dear."

I grinned.

"Maybe I'll do a mural on each of the children's walls."

"See," he said, picking me up by the waist and twirling me around again. "I knew you were brilliant."

I was out of breath and laughing when he set me back on my feet.

Then he kissed me and scattered all my thoughts to the wind.

I was the luckiest woman alive.

The luckiest of any woman in any century.

Keep Reading for a preview of CHAMPAGNE SILVER...

CHAMPAGNE SILVER PREVIEW

Chapter 1
Dakota Auclair

November 1868

"*I* do NOT need a husband."

I stood in my sister's mammoth dressing room with a hundred thousand yards of gold and white silk taffeta cascading around my waist to the floor.

I balanced on a little velvet platform with two seamstresses painstakingly measuring and pinning the hem of the dress. The taffeta rustled with each little movement.

My sister Bailey, big as a house—pregnant with her first child—sat on a blue velvet loveseat and grinned at me. She was positively glowing.

"Have a glass of champagne—for me—and enjoy yourself," she said. "You know I can't have champagne while I'm expecting."

Bailey's husband, Graham Daniels, insisted that she not touch a drop of alcohol while pregnant. To say that he was a hovering husband would be an understatement.

"These slippers are killing my feet," I said crossly. My sister insisted I wear the white leather lace-up boots for the fitting so that the length of the dress was perfect. The little one-inch heels would have been comfortable enough if they had been just a tad bit longer.

"I know," she said. "It's not my fault your foot is bigger than mine. Your boots will be ready in time for the ball tomorrow night."

The seamstresses did not complain as I shifted from one foot to the other, then steeled myself for the duration. Or a few more minutes, at least.

One of Bailey's ladies in waiting handed me a champagne flute. The bubbles always made me smile. It was, of course, the best. My sister had the best of everything. No exaggeration.

She lived in a house with eight bedrooms. Each bedroom had what she called an en suite with a bathtub and indoor plumbing.

Indoor plumbing was an unheard of luxury out here in the mountains near the little town of Whiskey Springs.

The house had a total of four stories. The entire top story was Bailey's studio for painting and sketching. Canvases stood on easels all around the room. Sometimes the paint fumes permeated the house all the way down to the first floor.

In truth, Bailey often took her canvases and paints outside or her sketchbook and charcoal pencils, but the studio was perfect for cold days and breathtaking views. Standing on the balcony outside her fourth-floor studio, in fact, we could see the town below us. And Graham swore he could see the lights of Denver from here, but I had never seen them. Bailey declined to comment.

"That dress is beautiful," Bailey said. "It makes you look like an empress."

"It seems far too extravagant for a mere masquerade ball."

"Maybe," Bailey admitted. "But isn't it fun? And since you're here to help me with the baby, the least I can do is to make sure you're happy."

"Your piano makes me plenty happy," I said, taking another sip of the smooth champagne.

We'd had a piano in Natchez, Mississippi, but when we had traveled west, we couldn't bring it. I think there were other reasons we had not brought it, but I had been too young to be included in that decision.

"Turn, just a little," one of the seamstresses said.

I turned, giving me a lovely view through one of the windows. A window in a dressing room.

The view, like all the views in the house was breathtaking. From here I could see the lawn at the back of the house.

"When did you build a gazebo?" I asked, watching as two men swept white paint on a freshly constructed gazebo.

"Oh that," Bailey said. "Graham had it built for the ball."

I started to ask why, then knew it was futile. Graham did things because he could. This gazebo looked more like a house. Flattened on the front with two French doors. It had glass windows and a steep roof.

Suitable for the climate, I mused, wondering if it had a fireplace, too, but I didn't see a chimney.

I twirled the stem of my glass and studied the clouds. It would be dark before long, but I could still see the clouds well enough. "It's going to snow," I said.

My brother, Colton, was the weather expert, but I had learned enough from him to know a few things about the weather. Besides, I had lived in the mountains for three years now. A girl learned a few things or two after that long.

Specifically, right now, I could tell by the way the clouds

hovered around the mountain peaks. When they moved up, there would be fresh snow on the peaks and this time of year, that snowfall usually spread to the foothills and valleys.

There were five of us siblings. I was second from the youngest. Bailey was second oldest.

Our brother was right between the four of us girls. A true middle child.

Somehow our parents had managed to have five children, one per year. Such precision.

"This is too pretty," I said. The bodice had a sweetheart neckline and long sleeves. More gold lace and layers upon layers, showing off my small waist and keeping my shoulders bare.

"Where else can I possibly wear it?"

Perhaps if I were going to a ball hosted by the Queen of England, then this would be the dress to wear. And even then, I would hope it did not outshine the queen herself.

"You can wear it anywhere," she said. "And if you happen to find a husband, then..." she shrugged and smiled mischievously.

"Please tell me you did not invite someone for me to meet." I narrowed my eyes at her.

"What makes you think I would do a thing like that?" She let her shawl drop off her shoulders and wiped her brow with a cool cloth.

Watching my sister go through these hot and cold flashes and every other miserable thing like waddling like a duck, made me think that not only did I not want a husband, but I also would think twice about having children.

"Because before you married Graham, you knew all the single men in town."

"I did not," Bailey said.

I just rolled my eyes at her. I loved my sister dearly, but she could not deny that she had a lot of beaus back in her day.

"I wouldn't do that," she said. "I would want you to have your own beau."

Not a hand-me-down. That notion was ingrained in all of us girls.

Our mother had always made sure that all of us, even the youngest, got new dresses each season. No hand-me-downs from older sisters, unless, of course, we just wanted something.

Mother had a strong sense of fairness that she had passed along to her offspring. We'd gotten fairness and kindness from her. We'd gotten fierce survivalness from our father.

Father had been killed in the war, though, and Mother had not survived long after we got the devastating news.

I was haunted by the loss of our parents. I had been young. Fifteen. And I still had nightmares. But I never told anyone that. Not even my sisters.

"What are you going to wear?" I asked, turning the conversation away from me.

"You'll see," she said. "I think you'll like it."

I just smiled. Out of us four girls, Bailey had always been the one who kept up with fashion.

So I knew that whatever she wore, even in her huge as a house state, she would look lovely.

"All finished, Miss Bailey," the head seamstress said.

"Thank goodness," I said, gathering up the skirts to step off the platform.

"Be careful, Miss," the seamstress warned. "The hem has a thousand pins in it."

"I will be careful." I walked straight to the loveseat and plopped down next to Bailey. Then I reached down, careful to avoid the pins, and pulled off the slippers that had been killing my feet for the last hour.

"It's a beautiful dress," I said adjusting the skirts around me.

"Maybe you should take it off so it doesn't get messed up," Bailey said.

I rolled my eyes, but I knew she was right.

Even if I didn't care about masked balls, particularly, it was hard not to be excited about a dress that was fit for an empress.

Chapter 2
Zachary Rivers
Present Time

"WE CAN'T SELL," Tiffany Auclair said, standing on the fourth floor balcony of the Daniels House.

"We have to sell, Tif," Hudson Auclair said, sweeping a hand across the view. "We have the opportunity to be set for life." Hudson looked over at me. "Right? Tell her Zachary."

I didn't get the chance to say anything. It was just as well. The biting wind had me too frozen through and through to give a coherent response anyway.

"We're set right now," Tiffany insisted.

Hudson put both gloved hands on his hips. "With the money, we can move away from here. We can go to New York. We can live someplace other than here."

I could see that this was going to take awhile.

They barely noticed when I opened the door and walked inside the large open top floor. What had started out as a studio for renowned landscape and wildlife artist Bailey Auclair, the original owner of the house, was now used for entertaining.

An outdoor grill had been installed as well as an outdoor fireplace.

Couches and chairs were scattered all around, inside and out.

I went to the gas fireplace and watched the flames licking at the faux logs. Much more efficient, but I personally would have left the fireplaces alone. There was nothing like the scent of wood burning in a fireplace on a cold night.

I hated to be part of what could easily turn into a rift between the two siblings.

My company, one of those big companies in one of those big cities that Hudson wanted to move to had sent me here for one reason and one reason only.

To acquire this house so they could turn it into a luxury hotel.

I could honestly understand both arguments. I could see Hudson's point. He wanted to take the millions and run. He was more of a male fashionista, not an outdoorsy type person. He didn't realize—or maybe he didn't care—that his money wouldn't last long in New York, but it wasn't my place to tell him.

I could see his sister's point, too. She was still young. She could still have a family. Still live here and enjoy this house that had been handed down through the generations that came before her. And Tiffany was an outdoorsy person. Still living in the house and working from home, she hiked almost every day.

And there was a third viewpoint. One that I had to concern myself with. As a hotel, thousands of people could enjoy this place every year. It could be a grand hotel, rivaling even THE Grand Hotel on Mackinac Island. Well, maybe not exactly, but in a different way. A much smaller scale.

I had to keep my eyes on that one. That was my job.

The door opened and the two siblings came inside. Tiffany went straight to the fireplace, holding her hands out to the warm flames.

"We decided to wait," Hudson said, going straight to the minibar and pouring himself a glass of wine. "We'll wait until after the fundraiser tomorrow before we decide. To give us time to sleep on it."

"Good choice," I said, although I saw it for what it was. It was stalling.

I could already predict the outcome.

They would sell. They would sell because Hudson was blinded by the dollar signs. And since he had moved away to Denver long ago, he didn't have the sentimentality for the area that Tiffany did.

I also knew that he would regret it one day. And if he didn't regret selling, he would regret strong arming his sister into it.

This place meant something to her. She had every right to keep it.

"If you'll excuse me," I said. "I have to go into town to pick up my tux."

I didn't tell them that I had three in my closet at my home in New York, but I hadn't foreseen the need to bring formal clothing to a house in the middle of the mountains.

Unfortunately, that put me over more in Hudson's camp. And I hated that.

I hated it because I agreed with Tiffany on just how beautiful and special this place was.

Thank God it ultimately wasn't my decision to make.

I honestly knew I would struggle with the decision. For me I would have to weigh in whether or not I would have heirs.

Tiffany and Hudson had no heirs. But they still had time.

In the meantime, I would be attending the fundraiser they were holding here tomorrow night. The fundraiser had nothing to do with the sale of the place, at least not directly. Indirectly, it had everything to do with it.

Tiffany had opened up the house to an art gallery in town raising money for a charity. Since this had been Bailey Auclair's home, it seemed appropriate to hold the fundraiser here. What I knew was that they were awarding Tiffany a fee for the venue.

The house was expensive to maintain and needed some work. That's where I came in.

The event was significant in that it might be the first of many such fundraisers to be held in what was currently known as the Daniels House. What was to become a destination called the Daniels House Hotel outside of the little town of Whiskey Springs.

I walked down to my room on the second floor.

Bailey Auclair must have set some kind of record on the number of paintings she had done. There was one on every wall. It was my understanding that they had been thinned out over the years. At one point the house was all but papered with them and she had painted a mural on in each of the five third floor bedrooms. The bedroom that had belonged to her five children.

Only one of those murals still existed. It was a lovely mountain scene with wildlife including a flying eagle, an elk, and chipmunks.

It would have been a travesty if they had painted over it.

It was a shame they had painted over any of them. They would be perfect for the hotel rooms.

It was a great loss.

But what was left could be protected.

If I did my job well enough.

Chapter 3
Dakota

THE COLD EARLY afternoon air kept the guests pressed inside.

I had been right. It was snowing. Beautiful, soft snowflakes.

Not a blizzard. So hopefully all the guests would be able to go home in the morning if not tonight.

Bailey and Graham had set up pallets on the second floor of the house for overnight guests.

But for now, guests were still spilling in. People wanted to see the house. I knew most people came for that, if nothing else.

I would not deny that the house was something to see. It was aglow with candle light. And the air was scented with fresh flowers everywhere. Daffodils. Poinsettias. Daisies.

A small four-man orchestra played in the ball room, providing what was supposed to be a joyful background.

I stood in the foyer next to my sister and Graham. There was a lull in the incoming guests, but another carriage was making its way up toward the front circle drive.

"I should go," I said to Bailey. "I don't have to meet everyone."

She put a hand on my arm. "Stay," she said. "I like having you here."

One of the guests came up to speak with Graham and the two men stepped away.

"See," she said. "You're keeping me from standing by myself."

"Very well," I said.

"Are your boots hurting your feet?" she asked.

"My boots are fine. I hardly notice them."

"What is it, then?"

"These people are all strangers to me," I said. "There were so many people, I could not remember their names if I'd had to.

"I don't know a lot of them either," Bailey said with a worried glance over her shoulder. "And I'm sure all of them were invited."

She looked back at me and smiled. "But we'll dance and enjoy the evening, right?"

"Of course," I said. But I knew our younger sister Elise would have been better at this. But Elise was at away at school. I was the only available sister to keep Bailey company.

"At least let me get you some punch," I said.

"Very well," she said. "As long as you get some for yourself as well."

I turned and took a step.

"And where's your dance card?" she asked.

I reached into my pocket and pulled out the little dance card I had hoped to keep hidden away. Held it up for her to see.

"Put it on," she said as I walked away.

So with that, I escaped the duty of greeting guests, at least for the moment.

My dress rustled as I navigated my way through the guests toward the refreshment table. My dress was by far the prettiest and more elegant than anyone else's.

Even my sister wore a sedate gown in a deep solid burgundy. A high neckline and long sleeve befitting a lady in her condition.

It made me wonder all the more what she was up to by outfitting me in such a lavish gown.

I had my suspicions to be sure, but so far, I'd seen no eligible bachelors that she might be thinking to introduce me to.

I had no interest in being courted by anyone right now. I had my winter planned out. Keep my sister company until the baby came. Then help her with the newborn. She had a full library of books that I looked forward to losing myself in.

It was going to be a long winter, snowed in up here on the mountain. But I didn't mind. I rather looked forward to it.

As long as we were snowed in, we had no social obligations. And that suited me just perfectly.

As I reached the refreshment area, one of Bailey's ladies in waiting handing me a glass of punch.

"I need one for my sister, too," I said.

"Nonsense," the woman, Anna, said. "I'll take it to her. You just enjoy yourself."

Before I could protest, Anna had already taken off on her singular purpose. Bailey hated when I called her personal maids ladies in waiting, but I found it quite descriptive.

It wasn't their fault. Bailey had a way that drew people to her. Not just men, but women as well. Men wanted to be around her and ladies wanted to be her.

I took the opportunity to walk down the wide hallway leading to the back of the house.

Although I had not lied about the boots not hurting my feet, I was quite tired from just standing for so long. Surely one of the ladies in waiting would bring her a chair.

Refusing to make it my problem, I sat on one of the little velvet benches.

It couldn't hurt to just take a break from everyone.

Keep Reading Champagne Silver...

Kathryn Kaleigh is the author of over seventy novels, over one hundred short stories, and many collections.

kathrynkaleigh.com